The Gunsmoke Serenade

Thomas McNulty

A Black Horse Western

ROBERT HALE

© Thomas McNulty 2016
First published in Great Britain 2016
Paperback edition 2019

ISBN 978-0-7198-2985-7

The Crowood Press
The Stable Block
Crowood Lane
Ramsbury
Marlborough
Wiltshire SN8 2HR

www.bhwesterns.com

Robert Hale is an imprint
of The Crowood Press

This book is dedicated to
My beautiful wife Jan
With all my love

Typeset by Catherine Williams, Knebworth
Printed and bound in Great Britain by
CPI Group (UK) Ltd, Croydon CR0 4YY

The Gunsmoke Serenade

ile passing through Cherrywood Crossing, US Marshal
field Knight is confronted by a gang of hired guns who tell
to ride the other way, or be shot down. With no choice but
de into the high country, Knight soon learns he is being
ted by a man named Silas Manchester, but why, he has no
Determined to survive this dangerous game that he's
forced to play, Knight is destined to become the hunter
r than the hunted.

ided by a mountain man named Lacroix, Knight decides
ing the fight to Manchester and get answers. Meanwhile,
ht's partner, Deputy US Marshal Cole Tibbs, sets out
ing for his missing friend. Tibbs will discover that he, like
riend, has also become part of a dangerous game that
into a serenade of violence.

ONE

The day after they hanged Cal Randal three strangers rode into town on black horses. That they were gunfighters was not in question, but it remained to be discovered if they were bounty hunters or outlaws. When Maxfield Knight saw them he was exiting the Springwater Saloon after a tumbler of whiskey had burned away the dust in his throat. He paused, pulled a thin cigar from his vest pocket, struck a wooden match on his trousers and exhaled a cloud of blue smoke into the dazzling sunlit street as the riders tethered their horses to a hitching post near the hotel. That his life was about to change was unknown to him, but his innate senses struck a warning that caused him to pause and study the three men for a span of perhaps two minutes.

Drifters and hired gunmen. They had Winchester rifles in their saddle boots and their horses were anything but fresh. Both men dressed plainly enough – brown trousers, checkered wool shirts, leather vests cut short above the gunbelt, the hard walnut grip of their Colts scarred with age, black Stetsons that shadowed their unshaven snarls – and the trail dust powdered them like a disease.

It may have been something in their look when the three

of them made eye contact that sent a warning signal to Knight's brain. It may have been the cold dark look a killer brings with him when he's sighted his prey that made Knight pause and stare back at them. Then the eye contact was broken and the two men paid him no further attention.

But there had been something ...

After they tethered their horses to a hitching rail and pulled their Winchesters from the saddleboots they ambled into the Constitution Hotel, where undoubtedly they would ask for a bath. Men on the trail hankered after a soiled dove for company and enough whiskey to dull the pain of their saddle sores, but no dove would dance with a man that smelled as bad as a mangy dog.

Knight continued on his way to the sheriff's office, where he found Luke Dobbs with his boots on his desk and reading a newspaper.

'There's coffee on the stove,' Dobbs said without looking up.

Knight took a tin cup from the table near the stove and poured himself a strong cup of Arbuckle's coffee. He took the chair opposite the desk.

'Three gunmen just rode into town,' Knight said.

'If they don't start anything I won't kill them.'

'Could be they're friends of Cal Randal.'

'Could be. Is Cole Tibbs still in town?'

'Nope, he went fishing after getting that telegram from his girl down in Raven Flats. She's a pretty thing named Jamie Hart.'

'They're all pretty when they're young.'

'Hell if they are,' Knight said, 'that girl slinging hash over at Tenney's Restaurant looks to be half buffalo.'

Dobbs laughed. 'It's more like she's half moose, and an old moose at that.'

Knight chuckled softly. 'You get any new Wanted dodgers?'

'The west is secure,' Dobbs intoned. He still hadn't looked up from his newspaper. 'Buffalo Bill made the west safe for us all. I read it right here in this newspaper not a month ago.'

Knight snorted derisively. 'Old Bill has found himself a way to line his purse with coins, hasn't he? I do admire that old coot.'

'He got out before he ended up like Hickok.'

'So the west is secure,' Knight said sarcastically as he finished his coffee, 'except someone forgot to tell those three gunmen that just rode into town.'

'Don't stir up any trouble,' Dobbs said.

But Knight had quietly set his cup down and was out the door. The day was warm and the sky a fragile blue. The town of Cherrywood Crossing was a tranquil place but Knight remembered a day all those years past when it hadn't been so tranquil. Coming back with Cal Randal had been something his job as a US marshal required. If not for that he never would have come, but Knight set his personal feelings aside and did his job.

Cal Randal had robbed a bank in Cherrywood Crossing a year before, been caught and sentenced to hang because a bank guard had been killed. Knight and Deputy US Marshal Cole Tibbs had caught up with Cal Randal at old man Saberhagen's farm and brought him back to town. Circuit Court Judge Augustus Fitzsimmons had sentenced Randal to hang and finally they did just that. Knight and Tibbs had supervised the hanging and observed the burial. Cal

Randal was in Boot Hill and Maxfield Knight was between assignments.

Hell, I should ride out now, Knight thought to himself. *Sheriff Dobbs doesn't need any help from me.*

Knight was no stranger to Colorado. He passed through Colorado several times a year, but seldom did he ride into Cherrywood Crossing. With whiskey in his belly and nothing much to do except wait for Tibbs he decided to take the ride that he'd been avoiding, but as his mind pondered the thought he found ways to postpone that ride.

Tibbs had gone fishing at the creek south of town. Knight considered joining him but then changed his mind. He returned to the Springwater Saloon, where he had another whiskey. Fifteen minutes later he joined three cowpunchers for a friendly, low stakes game of poker. They made a point of ribbing him about playing an honest game. They were good-natured cowboys and seemed to enjoy having a US marshal sit in with them.

'Now don't you pull any aces out from under that tin star,' one man said, grinning.

'Hell, I'm too old to pull anything like that on you boys.'

A low stakes poker game helped pass the afternoon. Looking back on it later he couldn't quite recall the names of his poker companions – maybe Bob, maybe John, maybe Andy – affable farmers. And maybe it was that extra glass of dark whiskey that contributed to a temporary feeling of peace. He won a few hands and lost more. But Knight was fine with losing a few dollars. Sometime later he thought he might ride out and find Tibbs at the creek. Maybe tomorrow. A day in the sun fishing a fast-running creek seemed about right.

At four o'clock that afternoon the three gunmen ambled into the Springwater Saloon. They sat high on wooden stools at the bar, their spurs jangling clumsily against the mahogany counter. One of the men bumped a spittoon and sent it rolling across the dusty floor.

It was the way their eyes pretended to casually mark his location that bothered him. They had left their Winchesters elsewhere, probably up in their rooms, but gunmen like these relied just as much on their Peacemakers. All three of them glanced at him as they seated themselves. It was as if they were of one mind, and Knight felt an intuitive alarm that he could never put into words.

He digested the fact that these three drifters were interested in him. He continued to play poker, his back wisely to the wall. He had instinctively chosen his seat carefully. From his position he had a direct line at the men, and they, in turn, watched him in the expansive mirror behind the bar.

They drank beer, and slowly. They appeared to be in no hurry. The barman paid no more attention to them than any other patrons. Knight counted the customers. The three drifters, his three poker companions, a soiled dove and a fat man drinking whiskey near the batwing doors. And the barman. It was a slow afternoon at the Springwater Saloon.

A fly buzzed past. Outside the street gave up the occasional sound of hoof beats or a wagon clattering along. When the cards were being shuffled Knight dropped his right hand down to his holster and gently plucked the leather thong from the hammer. He wanted his gun free.

He lost the next two hands. He was no longer concentrating on the cards. The game was a pretence as he studied his options. They had no clear view with his three poker buddies on each side. But if someone pulled a gun everyone would clear the table right quick. Knight didn't know how fast they were but that didn't bother him. He would kill all three quickly. What he wanted to know was why. Who were they?

None of the men looked familiar. They were young, mid-twenties, angry young men without education looking to make a name for themselves with a gun. But why were they after him? He supposed it was possible they were kin to someone he had killed. Maxfield Knight had lost track of how many men he had killed.

One of the men said to the barkeep, 'You got an outhouse?'

'Out back.'

The man got up, gave Knight a long look. Their eyes met and Knight held the man's stare. He held it and the man flinched, broke eye contact, and went out the rear door. When he returned a few minutes later he avoided looking at Knight.

Got him, Knight thought. *He'll be the first to draw.*

Then the man quickly finished his beer. He smacked his lips. He ordered another beer.

He's working up the courage now.

The other two hadn't finished their first beer yet. They both glanced over at Knight. They were all being open about it now, give him a look, fearless, size him up before they make their move.

Damn fool boys!

The man that was half through his second beer slid off the stool. He clenched his fist and opened his fist nervously.

'You boys set your cards down and get out of the line of fire,' Knight said softly.

At first his three companions seemed confused, but then they sensed what was about to happen. The drifter had come up near the table, his hand just inches from his holstered gun. The table cleared with a rush of squeaking chair legs, jangled spurs and Stetsons slapped hurriedly back on to their heads.

'I hear you're as fast as Hank Benteen,' the man said.

'Who sent you?'

That gave him pause. He seemed confused. He wasn't expecting the marshal to ask questions. Knight stood up and said, 'Do you really want to die today? Now tell me who sent you?'

The man looked back at his two friends. They scooted from their stools and fanned out, but far behind their brazen friend.

'I said I hear you're as fast as Hank Benteen,' The man repeated. 'I don't think you're that fast.'

'Don't do it, kid. I killed my first man before you were born and I don't suffer from poor eyesight like Wild Bill.'

The man groped for his gun, pulled it from its holster, but all too slowly.

With a blur of speed Knight's gun came up, hammer back, his finger curling on the trigger, and the barrel roared with flame and smoke. The thunderous detonation shook the room. The man slumped, a red flower blossoming on his shirt, his gun falling from his already twitching fingers. His lips pulled back as his eyes rolled to whites, a thin line of blood splaying from his tongue as he tried to talk. Knight's gun roared twice more as the man's lifeless body slammed to the floor. The other two men, caught foolishly in a game they could never win, seemed resigned to their fate as they nervously yanked their guns free. One man went down as a bullet turned his forehead into a pile of red cabbage; the other took a shot in the chest. He yowled in agony and fell writhing to the floor.

'Damn you fools!' Knight spat.

Knight approached cautiously. The third assailant was still alive, although just barely. He coughed foamy blood. The bullet had gone through his lungs. The man – *more of a kid*, Knight thought – looked pathetic. His hat was crushed under his head and his gunbelt was too loose. It had pulled up over his belt haphazardly, strung across his belly.

'Get … get … a … doctor …' the kid wheezed.

'No, you're going to die, kid,' Knight said without sympathy, 'now tell me who hired you?'

'Silas … Manchester …'

'Silas Manchester? Who the hell is that?'

But the kid was gone. Knight cursed and holstered his gun.

'Get the undertaker,' he said to the barman. 'I'll tell the sheriff.'

Knight pushed through the batwings and paused on the boardwalk. He pulled out his gun, punched out the spent shells and replaced them with fresh cartridges. He holstered the gun, his eyes sweeping up and down the street.

Sheriff Dobbs had moved his feet off the desktop and had tossed the newspaper aside. He was drinking a cup of coffee and cleaning his sawed-off shotgun with a cotton towel. Knight told him what happened.

'And you never heard of Silas Manchester?'

'No.'

'You killed all three after they pulled first?'

'Go ask the barkeep and those card players.'

'Hell, I believe you.'

'You can—'

'Sure, I know my job. I can send a few telegrams, see who this Silas Manchester is, if he's anybody.'

'He's someone that wants to kill me,' Knight said.

'And they found out you're not easy to kill. This Silas Manchester would have known that, you have a reputation, so they were testing you.'

'That's the way I figured it, too.'

'Send three cowpunchers desperate for money, tell them something like you're old and slow on the draw.'

'Pay them well and offer more.'

'Let's go see what we can learn.'

Knight followed Dobbs to the Bull's Head Rooming House, where the desk clerk gave Sheriff Dobbs three keys for their rooms after stating they had paid in silver coins. In each room they found a Winchester rifle and their saddle-bags. In each saddlebag they found one hundred dollars in silver coins. They went downstairs and sheriff Dobbs studied the registration book. The names meant nothing, they were three strangers that had taken a fool's errand and died for it. Their names only meant they would have something to paint on their crosses in Boot Hill.

'We'll put 'em on display,' Dobbs said, 'give 'em a two-day showing. Then we'll bury 'em.'

The undertaker had it done before sunset. They placed the three bodies in pine coffins and propped them outside the undertaker's office. They set torches out and lit oil lamps, which swung from a hook under the awning. Dobbs wanted any night riders coming into town to see the results of their folly. If Silas Manchester were nearby or had any other men nearby they would certainly learn about the killings soon enough.

Knight had a room at the Continental Hotel on the second floor. It was the better hotel in town but when he entered his room he wasn't thinking about the comfort of a soft mattress and feathered pillow. He tossed his hat on the bed-post and unbuckled his gunbelt. He tossed the gunbelt on to the bed but kept the Colt in his hand. He sat on the bed and checked the cartridges even though he knew he had just changed them.

He got up and turned down the oil lamp. He turned the wick so low only a faint glow emanated from the lamp, barely enough to light the room. Knight let his eyes adjust to the gloom. He waited until the sky was completely black and then he extinguished the lamp. With his eyes adjusted to the gloom he rose and pulled the curtains aside. The street was dark but for the yellow glow of light spilling from the saloons. Down on his left the torches near the coffins sent shadows cavorting across the pallid features of the dead. The night breeze tugged at the torch flames and the fire danced like an angry demon. The dead men stared into an abyss, their gray skin and sightless eyes reflecting the torches that appeared to gyrate with an unholy ecstasy.

Thirty minutes later two figures on horseback cantered into view and paused to stare at the coffins. Knight couldn't make out their faces. They had their backs to him and, even if they had turned in his direction, their dark Stetsons were pulled low on their brows. But they took a long hard look and then eased away, the slow thump of hoof beats fading down the street.

Knight strapped on his gunbelt, took his Stetson from the bed-post and went downstairs. Outside the hotel he glanced up the street but the riders had melted into the darkness. No matter. They wouldn't be difficult to find.

Silas Manchester was paying good money to start this, and it no longer mattered to Knight who Silas Manchester was or what he wanted. His immediate interest was to fight. Knight had worn a gun a long time and a man that wears a gun has to learn how to use it without hesitation. Knight was such a man, and he made no excuses for the men he had killed.

He strolled down the boardwalk, his senses alert. At the far end of the street was a saloon called Cattleman's Saloon. He had avoided it because of its reputation for watered down whiskey. But it was here that he found two horses tethered to a hitching rail.

He pushed past the batwings and made for the bar. The bar was no more than some planks of wood suspended between barrels. The two men were easy to pick out. They sat at a table with a soiled dove on each side of them. The girls were giggling and one of the men had his dusty arms around a dove, his hands groping. The dove pushed him away and said, 'Buy me a drink first! I don't cotton easily to a man that smells worse than a horse!'

The man backhanded the dove, the *smack!* echoing loudly in the small room.

Knight said, 'Buy her a drink and apologize to her.'

The two men paused and focused on Knight. He watched their eyes. In his peripheral vision he was aware of where their hands were, the position of their boots on the floor, but mostly he watched their eyes. The doves looked at Knight in astonishment. One of the girls slowly stood up and backed away. She stepped lightly backwards and finally settled on a spot at the furthest end of the room.

And their eyes picked out the US marshal's star on his vest, the Colt slung low in its holster on his right hip, the cold, predatory look in his eyes and the steadiness of his hands. Knight was tall and weathered but gave the appearance of being strong, which he was. His dark but silver-tinged mustache curled around his lips. Assessing his age was difficult.

The other dove, finally pushing herself away, stood up and stammered, 'That's all right m-mister, I … I don't need nothin'.' And she backed away as well to join her friend as a witness.

Neither man spoke. They were as if suddenly frozen in place, unable to act on their own behalf. Death stood before them and the singular fact of that moment was not lost to them.

'We haven't done nothin' wrong,' one of the men said.

'What does Silas Manchester want?' Knight asked. The surprise registered in their faces, but both men remained silent. 'All right,' Knight drawled, 'you'll tell me now or later, it's all the same to me.'

He strode forward and his gun was in his hand quickly, the barrel pointed at the closest man. Knight reached down and pulled the man's gun from its holster and stuck it in his belt. He waved his Colt at the second man, 'Hand it to me butt first.'

With both men disarmed he instructed them to stand and he marched them outside with their hands raised. One of the men, objecting to being treated roughly, turned and tried to ram his elbow at Knight but the marshal slammed his gun across the man's face and pistol-whipped him to his knees.

'Men like you belong under a headstone with the worms,' Knight said. 'Now get moving.'

There was no further protest as the men were herded into the jail. Sheriff Dobbs, having dozed off with his feet on his desk, rubbed his whiskered jaw and cursed as Knight stomped into the office.

'Two of Manchester's men,' Knight said. 'You boys introduce yourselves to the sheriff.'

Their names were Vinnie and Rick, and Rick began to protest at being struck by the marshal.

'We ain't done nothin' wrong! You got no cause to lock us up! It ain't right that I get whipped like that!'

But lock them up they did, each in his own cell in the rear of the building. Knight stood in the hallway looking in at them and said, 'When you get a notion to talk about Silas Manchester you can tell the sheriff here. Until then you're our guests.'

Even Sheriff Dobbs had to chuckle at that. Returning to the office Dobbs said, 'They'll be expecting breakfast in the morning and if I don't serve it they should talk then.'

'They're stubborn, but they'll talk. That silver in their pockets won't do them any good behind bars.'

'You got any idea what this is about yet?'

'Nope. But I expect in the next day or so we'll find out.'

On his way back to his hotel Knight paused on the boardwalk. Further down the street the torches flickered weirdly and yellow light dashed across the faces of the dead men in their coffins. The street was empty but for the vacant stare of those men on their way to their graves. The sky was too dark, too unyielding. It was as if a black curtain had been drawn across the sky and the air had been sucked from the earth. Knight felt closed in. He tried to shrug the feeling off but it lingered in his mind like the memory of a serpent's cold-blooded touch.

Back in his hotel room he sat on the bed's edge with his gun in his hand. How many times had he sat thus, waiting for the inevitable battle? He had lost count. His life had become an endless stream of gunfights. But he had no regrets.

He thought about her then and he knew in the morning he would take the ride that he'd been avoiding. It wasn't far. Just north as the crow flies. Many years ago it had been a pleasant valley bordered by mountains and forest. In the spring the birds sang in the trees and the brook was a good place to fish.

The gun was reassuring in his hand. The gun that defined him, the gun that was as much a part of Maxfield Knight as his own soul. Old Scratch might palaver a bit over the details but he had given it all up willingly that day long ago when he lost her.

Sleep was impossible. If he closed his eyes he was at Shiloh again because he could never leave Shiloh behind. It was always there, just as the burning of Atlanta was always with him; the stench of bodies burning on a pyre, the choking smoke, the sound of muskets volleying across the distant fields.

He set his Colt on the bed. The maid had pulled the blankets tight. The bed was a flat unruffled expanse that offered no comfort for a man suffering from insomnia. He paced the room. Finally, he turned the oil lamp down and extinguished the flame. His eyes had adjusted to the dark. There was a faint glow coming through the window from the street below. He looked out the window and nothing had changed. The dead men stared into eternity. The flames of the torches made dancing shadows. He checked his pocket watch. 12:45 a.m.

When dawn finally came he had dozed but a little, his mind thundering with echoes of battles long past. He heard a bird chirping outside the window. He went to the bureau and splashed water on his face from the basin. He dried his face with a small towel and strapped on his gunbelt. Picking up the Colt from the bed he holstered it and went downstairs to see about his horse.

An hour later he had ridden north following the creek that ran south past Cherrywood Crossing. The sky was a fragile shade of turquoise, the strips of small gray clouds hanging at the horizon reminding him of the gunsmoke that hung over the peach trees at Shiloh. He had come to Cherrywood Crossing with his wife after the war but the war had followed him even to this tranquil paradise. He rode with a solitary purpose and whatever emotions he felt were long buried and his granite features revealed not a hint of turmoil.

Across a pasture of green grass where once stood a small farmhouse and barn. Over a hill and alongside the creek and then he reined his horse to a halt. There had been something on the wind, he thought, or was it just a memory? The place was full of ghosts but perhaps he was too accustomed to their presence. It was true that there were times when the dead spoke to him with such conviction that he often failed to heed the words of the living.

Putting the spurs to his horse, he cantered along a deer trail and passed through a copse of trees and rode into another pasture. The morning sun beat at the grass and the grass swayed mockingly in the wind. The paint on the picket fence that surrounded the lone grave was peeled away by the sun, wind and rain. The little gate swung easily open and he stood there quietly for some time with his hat in his hands without speaking. He stared dully at the stone marker's simple words: MARTHA KNIGHT – BELOVED WIFE. Because she had died so young Knight often wondered how she might have reacted to the crow's feet that now tugged at his eyes and the salt and pepper slant to his hair.

There are tales of Maxfield Knight that are well known to cowhands and drifters who picked them up on cattle drives or in the saloons of faraway Dodge City, or as far south as San Antonio. Some of these tales were true; his gunfights with Jake Grimstone, Carleton Usher and his sons, and a legendary battle against Juno Eckstrom and his men at Crippled Horse. But of all the tales that none could verify was the story of how Maxfield Knight hunted down the men that had killed his wife while robbing the bank at Cherrywood Crossing. He had never spoken of it and none had been bold enough to ask.

After a while Knight nodded once to the gravestone and put on his hat. Striding from the grave he looked straight ahead, his face an unreadable enigma. He mounted his horse and gently tugged at the reins. He hadn't gone far when some innate sense warned him, but he continued on his way as if nothing was wrong. He wasn't surprised when the rider cantered on to the trail and stopped twenty yards ahead of him. There was nothing unusual about the man, no discerning features. He looked like any cowpuncher on the trail. The man held a Winchester across his legs but gave no outward sign of hostility.

'Who sent you?' Knight asked.

'It don't matter none right now,' the man said, 'so you best just ride up toward the mountains.'

'That's out of my way. I'm riding back to Cherrywood Crossing.'

'Not today.'

In a flash Knight's Colt was in his hand, the barrel pointed at the man's chest. The *click-clack* of a Winchester being loaded sounded on his right. Almost immediately a horse neighed on his left. A turn of his head in both directions revealed they had him surrounded. The men on each side of him had their rifles pointed at him. The man before him remained passive.

'You'll have a chance is all I can say. You gotta go up into that tree line yonder.'

'What's this all about?'

'We're giving you a chance to get on. You can see how it is. We get paid to tell you what direction to go. If you refuse we shoot you down, but we'll make more money if you skedaddle up thataway.'

'I'm a US marshal. You can't get away with this. You boys need to give this foolishness a rest and tell me who put you up to this.'

'We are being paid in gold by Mister Silas Manchester of Atlanta.'

'That name doesn't mean anything to me. He sent men into town that are dead now. You ponder that.'

'What matters is that your name means something to him.'

The man on his left fired once, the bullet striking the ground in front of Knight's horse and kicking up dirt. The horse, startled, almost bolted but Knight reined him down and said, 'Steady boy.'

'We've done enough talkin'. You get the idea. Now once you cross that line of trees past the meadow out yonder we are coming to kill you. That's your chance to get away.'

'You're hunting me?'

'Get going.'

Knight estimated his chances. Two of the three men had the better position. Instinctively he also knew there were more men out of sight. They had planned this well. And while the name of his enemy meant nothing to him, he embraced the hunt they had set before him. In the end he would know everything he needed to know about Mister Silas Manchester of Atlanta. His mouth twisted into an almost evil grin.

'I'll play your game,' Knight said, 'and I'll see you boys real soon.'

Slapping the reins, he spurred his horse into a run and made for the trees.

TWO

At sunrise the forests of summer are places of solitude. He had come to prefer the forests over the desert, although the desert of his youth and the town of Raven Flats would always have a special place in his heart. But a forest was something else to consider, and in his travels he had learned of the pleasures of trout fishing in a clear mountain brook. Deputy US Marshal Cole Tibbs was not a talented fisherman; not in the way the great anglers of Wyoming and Colorado were great, but he was capable. Sometimes being capable was all that a man owned.

Before the sun had crested the horizon he was at the edge of a clear running brook, the water rushing with a sound like a song that swept past and trickled out of view as the birds high in the pines whistled a lullaby that signaled the dawn. He had cut a fishing pole with his Bowie knife using a sapling branch. The green wood was flexible enough and wouldn't snap on him if he got tangled up. He used a store-bought hook that came from a Denver mercantile and a silk line from the same merchant. He had extra hooks and some old horsehair lines in his saddlebag. He didn't much care about the lures manufactured in faraway places like St Louis so he relied on worms and night crawlers he dug up from the moist soil. The day before he had caught two fish. He gutted them on the bank and tossed the entrails back into the water. He didn't want bears nosing in too close. He cooked the fish in a pan over an open fire and ate them all at once. There was nothing to match the taste of brook trout cleaned and cooked right at the edge of a cold-running stream.

It was idle time for him and he welcomed it. In the past year he had ridden alongside marshal Knight and faced down numerous adversaries, all of which can take a toll on a man's nerves. He had come to rely on his modest fishing expeditions as a useful way to relax and shake loose the trail dust. Some men preferred drinking in a saloon as their leisure activity, but Tibbs had limited his taste for whiskey to Christmas and his birthday.

His self-disciplined approach to life had given him a knowledge of the world that some would never understand. He was wary, cautious without being paranoid. Even here under the sun-baked forest that appeared so tranquil he knew danger could lurk at every turn. He wore his gun on his hip. His Winchester was loaded and always nearby. He surveyed the landscape periodically, squinting into the colorful hills for signs of riders.

On his third night he heard horses. Faint voices trailed off on the night wind. In the morning he circled his camp on foot but found nothing. He was in such a secluded spot that to find him would mean riding up to within twenty feet of him. He could see nothing looking up and down the stream because it curled off north and south of him. This was a stream that found its way by curling among the hills and trees by clawing its way south in a zig-zag pattern.

He set into his daily fishing routine and thought nothing further of the horses he'd heard. When the sun was high over the trees its rays cut across the stream and he could see the rocks and sand and the shadows of small fish as the water rushed headlong on its way south. A mile north of his campsite he had seen some prairie chickens. Wild chickens and hens were not uncommon but perished easily because of the profusion of cougars, bears and coyotes. He set out to catch one and found himself rewarded with two fresh chicken eggs. The chicken itself he caught and snapped its neck. Armed with a new meal, he returned to camp.

Tibbs gutted the chicken, plucked the feathers and tossed the entrails downstream. He cooked it on a spit that afternoon. The two eggs were broken into a pan and scrambled quickly with the tin fork in his saddlebag. The chicken was tasty although he wished he had some salt. He made a mental note to add salt to his war bag when he returned to Cherrywood Crossing. He ate the eggs and the chicken as the afternoon slipped into a tranquil sunset. The sky was awash with lavender and orange, burning at the horizon like a blacksmith's forge. This was the time of day he enjoyed the most. He had the steady sound of the stream to keep him company, the call of birds and the gentle breath of a warm wind to lull him to sleep. And he reveled in the way the light in a forest is changing constantly. The textures were vibrant; the pines swaying gently, their branches whispering ancient songs, a music of the west, rugged and mysterious.

The shadows lengthened as evening crept closer. He had decided that in the morning he would move his camp two miles north-east. There was a small lake that he found as he surveyed the area the previous week, and while he preferred river and creek fishing he thought the change of pace might get him some bigger fish. A freshwater lake with large bass and musky was quite a prospect for Tibbs. That night he watched the stars twinkling above and he wished his girl, Jamie Hart, was with him. He had been delaying any firm decision, but he reckoned at some point he would ask her to marry him. He slept soundly without a care in the world.

In the morning his horse was restless. The horse had plenty of grass to chew and he thought maybe they had been idle too long. He found the lake again easily enough. Rather than hobble his horse he let the paint amble about nuzzling the tall grass along the lakefront. He looked carefully for signs of life but the place was deserted. He did find old campsites, but months had passed since they'd been in use. There were no shacks or dwellings of any type around the lake. The lake itself was about sixty acres and he estimated its deep point was thirty feet. There were pines, maples and oak trees all around, but predominantly pines. So it was Pine Lake from that moment on.

He made camp, started a fire and made coffee. He had plenty of Arbuckle's coffee in a tin, and with the fish he caught and the prairie chickens he could survive all summer. Colorado was a world away from Arizona's deserts, but equally as breathtaking. After a few hours he was accustomed to the throaty birdsong that sprang up suddenly and added yet another texture to his splendid surroundings. Other than the many birds he saw only small chipmunks and squirrels, and the occasional hawk. No other wildlife was visible, although Tibbs knew these woods were home to many others.

That afternoon he witnessed a remarkable event. It was

early in the afternoon and the sky was a fragile blue color marked by only a hint of cumulus clouds in the west. He had a line in the lake and he'd been busy pulling in small bass. The bass were easy to gut and made about a silver dollar sized fillet. He determined to catch an even dozen for dinner, when a shadow flashed over the lake. He stood there transfixed as an eagle swooped down from its perch in a pine tree on the opposite shore, circled high once and then dove at the crystalline surface. There was barely a splash as the eagle's talons took a large squirming fish, and the eagle flapped heavily but swiftly and was gone into the treetops in an instant.

Tibbs was enthralled. Such a sight as watching an eagle take a fish from just below the surface of a hidden lake was tantamount to a religious experience. And, indeed, from a frontiersman's perspective such places were temples and all of the west was a rugged temple that tested a man's endurance, as well as his courage.

An hour later he heard gunfire in the distance. He could not be certain how close the shooters were, but they were quite some distance. The gunfire was faint, but plain enough. Sound echoes oddly though trees but he guessed they were several miles away. He couldn't be certain, but it sounded like revolver fire. There was a distinct difference in sound between a .45 Colt revolver and a Winchester or Henry rifle.

He was nestled on a cluster of trees that had fallen into the lake during a storm. The two trees had become a triangle with the center crisscrossed with small limbs. The overhanging trees made good cover for the fish that came in to feed along the shoreline. The lake was as clear as glass. He watched a school of small perch drift in and out of the rippling green shadows. The sun was hot on his back but his Stetson shaded his face. He was conscious of the weight of his holstered Colt on his right hip.

He knew the fish would be biting later in the afternoon. He pulled in his line and returned to his camp. He had built a fire back from the lake and under a circle of pines. From any angle he was nearly invisible unless someone walked right up to his camp. He had his horse hobbled twenty feet away eating from the grass in the clearing.

His rifle was propped against a tree. He lifted the rifle and levered the cartridges out, the brass spitting into the air and piling up on a patch of moss like glittering golden teeth. His mind was calm, although something nagged at him and soon he realized the sound of gunfire had bothered him. There were no farms nearby. There were no long stretches of pasture for cattle. Cherrywood Crossing and the surrounding area was isolated, twenty miles in any direction to another town. The land was good for farming but the railroad hadn't found its way here. A crop farmer could make something go with a garden and goats, chickens and pigs. Maxfield Knight had once owned a farm nearby. Could have been a drifter shooting his dinner. Could be.

He replaced the cartridges in his rifle. The breeze picked up and he smelled the pines and the clear, cold scent of a lake fed by a mountain stream. Maxfield Knight had never talked about what happened to his wife, and Tibbs had never asked. He heard the stories, but he let it go. A man's grief was his own business. The gunfire had made Tibbs think about a lot of things, and none of it was pleasant.

Through the trees he could see the whitecaps on the lake pick up when the breeze scuttled across the surface, the ripples flashing like small candles. He took the rifle with him when he walked away from his camp. He circled the lake on the south end, following animal trails. There was no sign of other men, not even Indian signs. He saw a groundhog and a porcupine. The birds seemed to follow him, chattering incessantly high in the branches. When he was at the halfway point he turned around and circled in the opposite direction. Satisfied that he remained isolated, he returned to camp and mused on gunfire while drinking a cup of Arbuckle's coffee from his tin cup.

He had lost track of the days. The mountains rose like a blue mirage above the treeline on the opposite shore. He was in the foothills of the Rocky Mountains and the lake was undoubtedly stream fed, nurtured by the melting snow that slid down the rocks every spring. He had found and enjoyed two good camps and he had the benefit of a natural food supply. He understood at least something of why Maxfield Knight had settled here with his wife after the war. He decided he would ask the ornery old coot about that, but it was probably wise to get a few snorts of whiskey into him first. Max Knight never gave any outward sign of sentiment, but he could strike as swift as a rattler, and without provocation. Tibbs considered it his good fortune that Knight was his friend.

Just before dark, when the forest was still and the fish were nipping at the insects that clustered at the water's surface; and when the twilight was easing through the trees to instill a calmness over the land, he heard a succession of rifle fire in the distance. The gunfire came from the west, at the ridgeline of foothills.

Although he was convinced that the gunfire had nothing

to do with Max Knight, he still couldn't shake that nagging thought. He packed up his gear. Whatever trouble was out there could best be avoided by traveling at twilight. Once he left his lakeside camp he would be on the open trail in thirty minutes.

The ride into Cherrywood Crossing was uneventful. There was no further sound of gunfire and the trail was lonely and dark. He couldn't help but think that he was leaving something special behind, and he vowed to find other such places. Camping, fishing and hunting suited him just fine. It was a big damn country, and the thought of his girl being with him in the future was a predominant image in his mind.

He knew something was wrong when he turned his horse on the main street of Cherrywood Crossing. The town was too quiet. Yellow light poured from the saloon but there was no laughter. He stopped at the sheriff's office and stared at the door. The place had been shot up. The glass was gone from the window and replaced with boards. His horse was nervous and nickered loudly and clomped a hoof. He dismounted and walked his horse to the water trough. Tying his horse to a hitching post, he walked up to the sheriff's office and called out, 'Hello sheriff Dobbs!' An interminable stretch of silence followed. He was about to shout again when the bullet-shattered door opened a sliver. Dobbs peeked out and then stepped on to the boardwalk.

Sheriff Dobbs had his arm in a sling and two days' growth of beard on his chin. The man looked like hell. He had a shotgun in his good hand.

'You took your sweet time getting back.'

'I didn't know I had to hurry.'

Dobbs shook his head mournfully. 'No, I guess you didn't

know. Not even a gypsy fortune teller could have seen this coming. You'd better come in. I have coffee on the stove.'

They sat at the desk with the door latched. A solitary oil lamp bathed the room in a golden glow. There were bullet holes in the walls. The cells were empty, the cell doors leaning open. Dobbs poured coffee into tin cups.

'I don't have any sugar.'

'This is fine.'

Dobbs took a sip, taking his time. He set the shotgun on his desk.

'You've been gone five days. They came two days ago and shot the place up. They took the prisoners and left me for dead.' Dobbs was blinking rapidly. It was obvious the man didn't enjoy telling it. He took another sip of coffee. 'I've been waiting to see what happens next. I sent some telegrams but I haven't had a response yet.'

Tibbs was impatient. 'Start at the beginning. Where's the marshal?'

'Don't know about the marshal, but it's a good guess he's in a tight spot.' Dobbs told Tibbs about the men the marshal had killed, and about Silas Manchester. 'And then the marshal rode out that morning. I haven't seen him since. Later that very day the men rode in and took back their own. They shot the hell out of this place. I'm lucky to be alive. I slipped out back when five of them with shotguns and rifles came through that door.' The sheriff's face had turned red.

'And you don't know any more about this Silas Manchester?'

'Not a damn thing. But somebody wants the marshal dead. I don't expect you'll ever see him again. This was all planned, and they knew who they were after. The only witnesses here are buried now. They broke their own men out of jail. Kid, I can't believe the marshal is alive.'

'Is that so?'

'Just don't get your hopes up.'

'I'll tell him you said hello.'

'What the hell does that mean? You got a plan?'

'A plan?'

'You have to have some kind of plan if you're going after those men. You'll need a posse.'

'The only plan I have is to keep my guns loaded. There's no other plan that works against men like that.'

'Well, you better make damn sure you know how to handle those guns. And I think you might do some praying, too.'

'You have any men in this town willing to ride on a posse?'

'Hell no.'

'So how am I supposed to get a posse together?'

'I can send a telegram up to Denver and ask the US Marshal's office for assistance. They haven't answered my last telegram, but I can send another.'

'That will take too long. Besides, I think the wires are down. I can buy extra cartridges and ride in an hour. It could take a week or longer before any other lawmen get out this far, and there's no guarantee on that.'

'And what can you and Max Knight do against a dozen men? Hell, this Manchester fellow might have an army out there. Even the fastest gun is only fast against one opponent, not a dozen.'

'Well, let's just say that I know Max fairly well. He's not going to roll over for these boys.'

'I'll send that telegram anyway. If you're so damn fool stubborn to go out there then I can have some say in making sure you get buried properly.'

'That's real kind of you.'

Tibbs left sheriff Dobbs shaking his head in disbelief. He went to the hotel and checked in. He had to wake up the disgruntled clerk, who had been sleeping behind the counter. All he needed was a few hours' sleep himself and he could be on the trail again before sunrise.

THREE

Maxfield Knight knew that at some point he would have to abandon his horse. The thought irked him. He had purchased the black sorrel but a few weeks ago. He hadn't named the horse but the previous owner had called her Mable. He thought that was a stupid name for a horse. Spinsters were called Mable, and maybe an old saloon girl, but not a horse. It was downright insulting. He decided if he gave her a name it might be Vendetta. He liked the word. Vendetta. It summed up things nicely. But now he was about to lose her. If they drove him above the treeline he would have to leave the horse behind.

He had lost them in the trees. They had fired on him but by then he was into a grove of aspens. He moved deeper into the forest and dismounted. He wanted to check his backtrail. The sun was going down and he had to be certain he had room to maneuver when nightfall came. And so all of the sad days of his life came down to this one moment where he crouched among the whispering pines on a mountainside with a Winchester and waited for his pursuers to come so that he might kill them. Knight was a man who was constantly aware of his destiny, but on this day he felt confident that destiny was postponed. He was too angry to die. And he had questions that he wanted answered. Those men had made a mistake, although they didn't know it yet.

They had pursued him to the trees, but then stopped. He had a sense they were sizing him up, or testing him in some way. They had said they would kill him after he reached a certain point and that meant they were hunting him. What grudge they held against him he could not fathom, but he wasn't going to be hunted down easily. The gold of Silas Manchester of Atlanta was motivation enough for these men. Knight would have to get to Manchester himself to get answers. He deemed that as his biggest challenge.

He surveyed his surroundings. He was in the foothills and deep in the trees. Everything went up from this point onward. The trails and switchbacks all climbed steadily into the Rockies. A mountain man who knew the area could stay hidden a very long time. Knight could chance it, and wait them out from some hidden place, but that wasn't his nature. And they knew that. He realized they expected him to strike back. Perhaps killing him was their only goal. The hunt was just a game to entertain them.

He decided to abandon his horse immediately. They would expect him to stay in the saddle and work north or south to get around them. Due west took him above the treeline, where he would be the most vulnerable. In order to survive he would have to do what wasn't expected, or at least give them that impression. He had to keep them guessing.

He unsaddled the horse and hid the saddle in some scrub brush. He took his Winchester from the saddle boot and the extra box of cartridges from his saddlebag. He had extra matches in his saddlebag too, so he took them as well. He loaded the Winchester. He had the Colt on his hip, his rifle, a Bowie knife on his belt, and plenty of ammunition. As an afterthought he took his bedroll, which had a slicker rolled into it. The mountains got cold at night. He felt invincible with all of this gear. Those men were truly damn fools for not killing him at the start.

He put his hand under the horse's nose and let her sniff him, and then he scratched up by her ears. He patted her neck gently.

'I expect they'll look after you. A horse means money. I'll come and get you later.'

He walked away without another word. He wanted to get up higher into the rocks. He picked a trail that went straight up. He made good time, moving easily even with all of his gear. The sun was dropping fast and the long shadows soon made it difficult to see. When night came in the wilderness it was an impenetrable wall of blackness.

He found a place on a switchback where he could see north and south and a good way down the trail that he'd followed. There was plenty of cover.

Knight knew from experience that life in the mountains was challenging, but tranquil too. At sunset the wind brings songs to the pines and the light is everchanging. The spirits of explorers and early settlers are but a step away. The forest changes in late afternoon. The colors deepen as the shadows crawl out from beneath the underbrush. The pines and the wind are conspirators at twilight, telling stories of days past and greeting the future with a lullaby of whispers.

Some short time later he saw smoke drift across the high trees two hundred yards down the trail. The smoke was like a gray wraith against the vibrant green of the pines, and then it dissipated. That was the first camp. Within thirty minutes he found two more. The furthest camp was probably the main camp and would be heavily guarded. The other two camps were set on either side of him. So they had formed a triangle with two front guards. Those men would be the first to hunt him come morning.

He was besieged by mosquitoes when the sun was a red molten orb at the treeline. Glancing up at the encroaching darkness, he knew he could disappear into the forest. They knew it, too. This entire game was proceeding on the principle that he would not run. They knew this as much as he did. He would not run. The forest path and the mountains offered sanctuary for a man like Knight determined to stay alive. But they knew he wouldn't run. So it came down to fighting and discovering why. The goal now was to stay alive and to find out what this was about, and then take as many of them down as he could manage.

When the darkness was complete he began his descent down the trail. He aimed for the camp on his left, taking with him only his Colt and the Bowie knife. He left his rifle back up the trail hidden in a rocky crevice. He had removed his spurs and left them near his rifle. His eyes adjusted to the dark and he moved carefully to avoid making any sound.

When he had reached a certain point, he paused. There was no sound but the whispering pines and the faraway hoot of an owl. He was alert and feeling strong. Fatigue had not struck him yet. The thought of getting tired never bothered him. He had no shortage of places to hide and rest. This, he thought, was a tactical error on their part. He would have to exploit it.

After some time he smelled tobacco. He moved toward

the smell. The sentry was smoking a cheroot and in the faint glow from the burning tobacco a clear view revealed he had placed his rifle against a tree trunk. With the Bowie knife in his hand, Knight couched in the darkness and considered his attack. There was no way to get around the man. This would have to be a frontal assault, carried out swiftly, and with minimum noise. When he had it clear in his mind he moved as close as possible.

Twenty feet. Too long a distance, he thought. How fast could he move? The crackle of his boots in the underbrush would give him away immediately. He edged closer, stepping carefully. When the sentry took a drag on his cheroot the glow lit up his face. He was young, too young. No more than a boy. Knight had seen boys this age die before. He had killed a few of them himself.

The lead that flew through the air at Shiloh sounded like locusts taken to wing. That had been his first taste of battle and his first taste of death. The green earth was littered with the bodies of young boys, their faces like cherubs shattered by a musket ball. He stood silently and watched this young boy smoke, his skin smooth and unblemished, the glow from his cheroot catching the boyish curls that jutted out from his Stetson. *What the need for money did to men was a sin in itself,* he thought. Knight felt that he was caught up in circumstances beyond his control.

Just a damn kid. How many were young like this? Knight resisted the urge to curse under his breath. Then, making his decision, he leaped forward and clubbed the kid with the butt of his knife, knocking him senseless.

The other sentry, hearing the boy fall, said: 'Hey Billy, did you hear that?'

Knight was jumping into the darkness, racing at the other guard and knocking him senseless too before he could utter another word. He stripped both unconscious boys of their guns and retreated into the dark forest.

Many men feared the darkness. To some the forest's pitch black night was unbearable, but Knight had learned to embrace the darkness. More importantly, he had trained himself to find his way through the Stygian darkness by relying on his senses. Ignoring the mosquitoes and gnats that flicked about his head, he pressed on until he was a good distance from the camp of his pursuers.

He also realized his tracks would be easy to find once the sun was up. His best hope now was to get into those high rocks just below the treeline and wait out the night. In the morning he would have to skedaddle until he could find a way to make sense of his predicament.

He marked his path by the stars, working in a loose pattern to the north. Finally he came to a small section of rocks that took him up a switchback that might once have been a burro trail made by miners. He set down the holsters he had taken from the two boys. The extra guns and cartridges would be useful. He didn't yet feel any overt sense of fear, although he was perplexed as to why he was being pursued. *Everything will be made clear in due time*, he thought.

It was pitch black in the forest and he couldn't see his hand in front of his face. Then he heard a wolf howl in the distance, but close enough to be a concern. Another wolf answered the call. Maxfield Knight begrudgingly accepted that he might be pursued by more than just gunmen.

The mountains echoed the ominous howling of the wolves.

FOUR

He awoke to paradise.

A small bluebird chirped merrily on a branch. High in the sky he tracked an eagle soaring on the wind and circling, its white feathered head catching the sun. He studied on the eagle's path and, scooping up the extra holsters, he made his way along the trail still moving north. He had slept fitfully, one eye wary of any wolves that might sneak in on him. They certainly had his scent, but whether they would decide to hunt him down was a matter of speculation. Wolves could be unpredictable, and hunger was enough by itself to encourage a wolf pack to hunt and kill a man. They could do so quite easily.

Down the long trail he heard voices and he knew his pursuers were up and after him. He moved along the treeline in a straight enough manner, careful where he stepped and keeping to the rocks. If they were good trackers they would be able to guess where he spent the night, but that process could take several hours. He wanted to put as much distance behind him when they arrived at their conclusion. His goal was for them to be uncertain what direction he had gone.

The sun lit up the spruce and pine trees, casting green

shadows over the pale boulders. It was going to be a hot day and he was already sweating. A hour later he stopped to rest and listen for any sound of his pursuers, but his backtrail was quiet. Still, those wolf howls the previous night had set him on edge. A hungry wolfpack was the last thing he needed to worry about, but experience had taught him there was no such thing as a leisurely walk in the Rocky Mountains.

Climbing on to a boulder he looked down at the green valley where a small lake glimmered in the morning breeze. He estimated the lake was about ninety acres and ringed by tall pines. There were no signs of cabins, but that didn't surprise him. The Rockies were dotted with secret lakes and unexplored valleys known but to few. This was a place seen by Indians and mountain men, trappers and fur traders. It was harsh country for an average man to handle, and only the stoutest of men might survive the brutal winters.

Maxfield Knight never considered that the odds were against him. Even with a platoon of pursuers on his trail he was confident of staying alive. He had plenty of ammunition and he was secure in believing if things went bad for him that he could still escape and hide in these labyrinthine hills.

He pondered the lake for some time and studied the surrounding area. There was some marsh land south of the lake that he would have to avoid. He didn't want to get pinned down. But he thought he might use the landscape to his advantage.

Voices drifted on the breeze. Looking down to his right and far south of the lake, he spotted men on foot and some on horseback. They were spread out in thirty foot increments as they searched for him. He counted twelve men. They were being meticulous and taking their time.

Another sound caught his attention and, craning his head to the north-east, he counted eight additional men searching for him. That meant at least twenty men were spread out and hunting him down. He was a little surprised by that, but his analytical mind instead focused on keeping them at a distance rather than giving in to fear.

He resumed his study of the lake. On the western and northern shore there were several small bays where the shoreline was covered in scrub brush and some fallen old birch trees.

The nearby yapping of wolves behind him forced him to swing his Winchester around and scrutinize the timberline. A prickly sensation spread across his flesh as the wolves yapped again, this time much closer. If they came at him from above they would force him in the direction of the hunters. Even more disturbing was the fact that if Knight used his rifle to protect himself against the wolves it would reveal his location.

With limited options he continued north along the faint trail that had dwindled to a thin line used only by deer or raccoons. Twenty minutes later he hadn't heard the wolves yapping again but he felt something pinching his leg persistently. He stopped knowing what it was. Yanking off his boot he rolled up his trouser leg and found two fat ticks with their heads already imbedded in his swollen flesh. Knight cursed. Ticks were all too common in the woodlands but these two had burrowed deep. He would have to burn them out.

Retrieving his wooden matchsticks from his vest, he struck one against his boot and held the flickering flame up to the first tick. It squirmed and backed up, wriggling free.

Before the match burned low he repeated the process on the second tick. He didn't care to waste his matchsticks on ticks. His skin was swollen where the ticks had burrowed in. A bubble of blood slipped off his purple wound and shattered on the dusty path. Knight cursed again. The wolves would smell even a small drop of blood. Slipping his boot back on he scraped the blood deeply into the dirt hoping to obliterate his scent.

Paradise was a deceptive place, he thought. A man could get killed by the smallest mistake. Pushing himself along a trail bordered by sun-blasted rocks, Knight was careful of keeping well below the treeline. It wouldn't do to be seen out in the open.

Crossing a swell dappled with sunlight, he stopped when he saw the wolf thirty feet ahead of him. He knew the look a wolf gets in its eye before it attacks, and this wolf was no exception. Something moved high up on his left but he dared not take his eyes from the wolf. Baring its teeth, the wolf crouched and sprang forward. Knight had just brought his Winchester up and sighted down the barrel when an arrow took the wolf in the ribs, spinning it around. Only a few seconds passed before a second arrow cut into the wolf's neck, jutting from the other side. The wolf flopped over, twitching, its breath coming in hard gasps before it twitched its last.

Knight spun to his left expecting to see a Sioux brave, but the sight that greeted him was a surprise. The heavy man wearing a coonskin cap and buckskin shirt holding the bow, a quiver of arrows slung over one shoulder and an old flintlock rifle slung across the other shoulder, grinned at him from beneath a bushy black beard speckled with gray. His eyes shone mischievously.

'Now don't get your spurs all tangled up, mister. Just take it easy a moment and stay quiet.'

The big man hefted himself off the boulder where he had been perched and climbed easily down the trail to stand over the dead wolf. Knight was impressed at how easily the big man moved. He was light on his feet, and very quick.

'This is a good pelt. We'll take it with us. Quick now, we don't have much time.'

Handing Knight his bow, the man produced a foot long rope from his quiver and swiftly tied the wolf's front legs. When he was finished he scrutinized Knight, his eyes resting on the US marshal's badge pinned to his vest.

'A lawman. Well, you've brought a wagon full of trouble to these mountains. Seems like half the hired guns in the country are on your backtrail.'

'I was in Cherrywood Crossing and ...'

The man held up his palm. 'Later. Come on.'

Pulling the wolf, he turned on his heels and made his way up the hill, where they found another trail that ran parallel with the one Knight had been following. Presently they edged up toward some high rocks that were invisible from below because of the scrub and pines that clustered about the boulders. The big man gestured at the rocks.

'You see this?' He retrieved a rope that hung from an opening twenty feet above them. 'I use it because I'm fat. Time was I could use the hand holds and foot holds made by Indians in times past. Either way, we have to go up.'

To Knight's astonishment the big man placed one foot on a boulder and in seconds had hauled himself into the cave with the wolf dangling from the rope he now had clenched in his gleaming teeth. The man's voice boomed down: 'Haul your ass up here! Daylight's burning!'

Knight climbed swiftly but not with the same ease as this big mountain man, who greeted him again with a smile as he crawled into the cave.

'Pull that rope in behind you. No sense in giving those boys any clues whatsoever, no sir! They'll think you've flown into the sky!' The big man chuckled.

'I'm indebted to you,' Knight said.

The big man held out a meaty hand for Knight to shake. 'Albert Lacroix, son of Charles Lacroix deceased these past twenty years. I'm the last surviving son of Charles Lacroix, a mountain man himself.'

'I see.' Knight paused. 'I'm US Marshal Maxfield Knight. I sincerely appreciate your help out there.'

'Glad to be of service, yes sir!'

Knight looked around. The cave opening was small but fifteen feet inside and the cavern opened up so that a man could stand. It was too dark to see how far back the cavern stretched into the mountain. In the dim light at the entrance he saw some old stick figure paintings on the wall, and Lacroix had a large stack of skinned animal pelts stacked nearby. The pelts were worth a good sum down in the river towns.

'This is a tidy place to hide.'

'The Indians know I'm here,' Lacroix said, 'but they're finished since Buffalo Bill killed Yellow Hand years back to send a message about Custer. We don't have anything to worry about. We can even cook here because the smoke blows up a natural funnel and those high winds come in from the north and spread the smoke east. It's impossible to find this place.'

Knight noticed that further back there was a fire pit already stacked with fresh wood and a skinned rabbit on a stick braced over the pit.

'You've got a regular hotel here.'

'Oh, she's a fine hotel!' Lacroix chuckled again. His laughter was appealing, and while Knight had to admit the man was a bit eccentric, he accepted that eccentricity as part of a mountain man's solitary life. 'Now why don't you tell me about the trouble that's after you?'

Knight had no choice but to tell Lacroix what had happened, so he started at the beginning after they hanged Cal Randal. When he was finished, Lacroix whistled between his teeth.

'Damn, boy! That is something! I can say they moved in here about five days ago, way down in the valley where they camped in the prairie grass.'

'Do you know how many men there are?'

'Fifty at least, no more. They have extra horses and a wagon of supplies. They brought plenty of food. I could smell the beans cooking at night.'

'But you don't know who they are, or who their leader is?'

'Nope, I haven't got that close to them.'

Knight nodded. 'I'll set out before sunrise. I'm sorry if I brought any trouble your way.'

'Hold on now. Don't be so hasty and go get yourself killed. I might be of some use to you. Let's think on it tonight and talk in the morning. Meantime, you can help me skin this wolf.'

Knight had to unravel the extra holsters he'd wrapped about his shoulders, and unbuckled his own holster and set his rifle with his gear near the cave's opening. His bedroll had been strung on his back like a pack and when he was free of all that weight he felt himself relax somewhat.

'I've got some matchsticks and extra cartridges I can spare,' Knight offered.

'That's right kind of you but Old Betsy there uses powder and ball. I've got plenty and she still shoots true.'

As Knight expected, Lacroix was adept at skinning the wolf. Making his initial cut with his Bowie knife, he had the skin peeled back from the flesh and stripped the animal in mere minutes. 'I don't much like wolf meat,' he explained, 'so I'm not saving the carcass. Later tonight I'll take it down near the stream that flows into the lake and leave it for the bears. There's no shortage of game we can eat. You can see that I have a nice rabbit for our supper.'

He set the fur over a boulder near the entrance where the light was better and starting peeling the flesh off the underside with a large flint.

'That's a handy flint,' Knight said. 'Did you make it?'

'That I did. I learned how to make arrowheads and skinning flints from my pappy, Charles Lacroix.'

Knight nodded. The way Lacroix said his father's name was touching. His voice was filled with pride and it was obvious he missed his old man.

'You ever been married?'

Lacroix laughed heartily. 'That I was once, some years back. She was a half-breed Sioux women they called Tall Bird. She died in her sleep south of here one winter. This is no place for a woman, not even an Injun woman.'

Lacroix took the skinned but otherwise complete carcass and left it near the cave entrance. 'It's gonna swell and stink by sunset but we can't take a chance drawing attention to this area. Like I said, I'll take it out tonight.'

'Reckon I'll go along if that's not a bother to you. I'd like to look about.'

'I thought you might. We'll see what we can see and make some type of plan.'

Lacroix cooked the rabbit over his fire and Knight looked around in the glow of the flames. The mountain man had pelts stacked away from the entrance and an ample supply of firewood already cut. Lacroix explained that he cut the firewood outside and hauled it up in a burlap sack. He liked to have two weeks of wood already cut, but in the winter he had a month's supply in the cave and another month hidden down below. He was constantly cutting wood. Knight noted he had a short-handled axe and a long-handled axe, two flintlock rifles, an 1851 Navy Colt, a sack of gunpowder and a box of percussion caps and lead balls. Lacroix also had nearly fifty arrows already made. The man was prepared for anything, but Knight wondered if he was prepared for the trouble that had followed him into this mountain valley.

'Fire and fresh water are the two life giving things here in the mountains. I can hunt deer, bear, elk, rabbits, and beaver and live off the meat. I know a place where wild onions grow. I can sell furs in town if I need something more. It's a good life.'

They ate the rabbit and Lacroix made coffee. Knight counted his blessings. Pure luck had brought him into contact with this mountain man and changed the way Knight would handle his pursuers.

Knight sat at the cave entrance and looked out. His view was mostly obstructed by tall trees. Only someone stumbling up close to the cliff face would see the cave, but entering it would require strenuous climbing. Obviously defending the cave was easy. Still, Lacroix would want his home kept a secret.

There was no sound from his pursuers as the sun set. They waited until the sky was lavender before tossing out the rope and climbing down. Knight wore only his Colt on his hip, leaving his Winchester and extra six-shooters with his bedroll. Lacroix carried the Navy Colt in a holster and had his bow and quiver slung over his shoulder. Their goal wasn't to attack anyone, but simply to look around. Lacroix had tossed the wolf carcass out and hauled it by the rope cinched around the wolf's paws. Flies buzzed around the carcass as they made their way down the trail.

They moved silently and swiftly. Knight relied on Lacroix's knowledge of the area and followed him without much concern. The big man moved with the grace of a lighter man. Knight estimated they had traveled three miles from the cave when he heard the sound of water rushing over the rocks of a mountain stream. Lacroix untied the wolf carcass and left the body under some scrub brush where the bears would find it easily.

'Let's skedaddle,' Lacroix urged, 'I saw some grizzly tracks down here not even two days ago.'

The fading light had turned the sky red and yellow. A final burst of sunlight slashed through the trees and illuminated the trail before them. Once the sun dropped below the mountains the light would fade quickly and they would find themselves on a midnight trail where one mistake could get them killed. Knight, however, was only faintly concerned. He had faith in Lacroix. The man had survived dozens of midnight dangers, Indians, and brutal winters.

Continuing slowly, Lacroix eventually gestured that they stop. He pointed down the sloping trail. Following his gaze, Knight saw the lake he had noticed earlier. They were very close. Leaning close to his ear, Lacroix said, 'They have another small camp on the east shore. I reckon we can spook them tonight.' Lacroix patted his bow affectionately.

He followed Lacroix down to the lake's shoreline. 'There's an island around the bay on the far side. We can't see if from here. I have a canoe down here that we can use if she still holds water.'

The old bark canoe was secluded in brambles and branches and looked tight and worthy. Nearby a stream gurgled along and Lacroix mentioned the stream could be picked up in the hills. They pulled the canoe free and climbed in. Lacroix took the paddle and pushed them away from shore. He rowed silently and with great strength. The canoe sat low in the water because of their combined weight but Lacroix seemed unconcerned. They sliced through the dark blue water and the only sound was the whisper of the water and the paddle dipping below the surface. They would have been visible from shore, but again Lacroix seemed unconcerned.

The shoreline was dark and the horizon was fading fast. When they reached a peninsula Lacroix said, 'There's another bay around the left that ends near the marsh. Those men are camped near the marsh, but we're getting off here.'

Knight realized that the other bay hadn't been visible to him when he first spotted the lake because of an optical illusion. This peninsula jutting out from the eastern shore was only about forty feet across and seen from above the treeline had blended together to the naked eye. They beached the canoe and pushed into a strand of birch and spruce.

'What are you planning now?' Knight asked.

Lacroix grinned and patted his bow affectionately. 'Let's give those boys a real Rocky Mountain welcome!'

FIVE

When darkness fell in the mountains it was as ominous as a grave.

A lone owl hooted and the wolves yipped in the deep groves.

The earth turned and the lavender sky gave up its stars. Down near the marsh and settled on a patch of mossy earth, a campfire burned like a beacon. Voices drifted up from the camp. Idle talk of loose women and epic poker games. There was talk of cattledrives and gunmen like Hank Benteen or Chance Sonnet, legends of the west whose stories helped pass the time in many a camp. Mostly they talked about money and how they planned on spending it.

Knight counted eight men. Lacroix said they had one more further back on a trail to keep watch. He said he could sense him. Knight strained his eyes but he still only saw eight men, although he didn't doubt Lacroix. If he said they had nine men at this camp then it was nine men.

'I want the man on the trail,' Lacroix said.

'But we can't see him.'

'We will when he smokes.'

'You're betting he has tobacco on him?'

Lacroix nodded. 'Wouldn't you make sure you have tobacco on watch? It'll keep a man awake and help pass the time.'

They cut around a copse of trees and circled east. They saw nothing but could still hear the men talking in the camp. The fire crackled and smoke drifted on the wind. When Lacroix stopped they peered into the blackest part of the trail and still saw nothing. Lacroix pulled an arrow from his quiver and strung the shaft to his bow.

Knight smelled the tobacco before they saw it. An orange glow lit up the man's features as he inhaled on his quirly. Lacroix let the arrow fly and they heard it *thunk!* into the man's chest. He coughed, and then the tobacco was dropped and they saw nothing. They heard the man's death rattle and gurgling.

Satisfied, Lacroix turned and retraced their steps. They went a hundred yards and came to a spot where they could watch the camp. Neither of them spoke. Two of the men had fallen asleep.

Lacroix, tilting his head as if he heard something, whispered, 'Stay here a moment.'

Knight waited and listened while watching the camp. The conversation was dying down but there was still movement among the men. He heard Lacroix rummaging about in a thicket and worried the men in camp might hear it. This, however, was followed by silence. A few moments later, Knight heard a faint buzzing sound coming toward him. Turning around on his haunches, he observed Lacroix moving quickly in his direction. The buzzing sound grew louder.

'Stay put!' Lacroix rasped. 'I've got a hornet's nest!'

Faintly, Knight could see the buzzing round nest hanging

from a tree branch that Lacroix now held in his hands. With a mighty swing Lacroix heaved the nest high into the air, where it tumbled into the camp landing on one of the sleeping men. There was an instantaneous flurry of activity followed by loud curses that grew in intensity as the hornets went to work on the unsuspecting men.

Lacroix, seeing an opportunity to add to the mayhem, once again lifted his bow and let an arrow whiz at a man flapping his arms in a strange dance of consternation. The arrow punctured his chest and the man coughed blood almost instantly before falling in a heap. Shouts rang out. 'Indians! Damn it to hell, someone get help!' One of the men raised his Winchester and fired futilely into the darkness beyond the campfire's glow.

'That'll do it for tonight,' Lacroix said. 'That shooting will bring the others right quick. Let's skedaddle.'

They were in the canoe and paddling across the lake in minutes. Fifteen minutes later they looked back from the top of a hill and saw a line of torches marching in file through the darkness. The men were eerily quiet but Knight and Lacroix knew that didn't make them any less dangerous. By the time they reached the cliff below Lacroix's cave they heard a few Winchester shots, which they guessed were exploratory in nature.

Up in the cave they sat near the opening but the men brandishing torches never came near them, and there was no further gunfire. Knight realized that he was exhausted. The long day had taken his energy and he was grateful to curl up in a soft bear hide that Lacroix tossed in his direction.

But Knight had strange dreams. A boy at Shiloh emerged from the fog, his face eaten away by maggots, a bullet hole in his brow. The boy pointed a finger at Knight and smiled a death's head grin. Then Knight was running through the fog, but he couldn't catch his breath. His legs felt as if they were weighted down with lead. Dark shapes flitted in and out of his peripheral vision.

He awoke several times and stared at the cave's black ceiling. Lacroix was snoring contentedly. Knight admired the man's self-sufficient lifestyle and calm demeanour.

In the morning they chose to remain in the cave and sat near the edge to keep an eye out for intruders. Although their view was partially obstructed by a strand of pine, they could see a fair distance down-slope toward the switchbacks that curled east and west. They heard voices in the distance but no gunfire. Without knowing their adversaries true nature they were forced to guess at what might be happening. Knight conjectured that believing an Indian attack had occurred last night might force them to reconnoitre and perhaps even change their picket lines.

Lacroix observed that, having planned so well, their leader appeared to be the type to have a contingency plan. They weren't hunting without purpose, and they had planned well and at a great expense. 'You've got one devilish enemy down there,' Lacroix said. 'Besides, it won't take them long to figure there aren't any Injuns hereabouts.'

Shortly after noon they heard voices down below, possibly fifty feet away, but they never saw anyone. They spent time skinning a wild turkey that Lacroix had killed a few days earlier, and it was getting a bit gamey so Knight helped him skin it and cook it. After eating it Lacroix brought out his secret bottle of Tennessee whiskey, the best, he said, in any part of the country. Knight indulged himself with but a few swallows. The warmth slammed into him and spread through his veins. *That was enough*, he thought.

Once again they watched the light change the trees and the mountain colors stood out in contrast to the tumbling sky. Suddenly they heard a sound that caught their attention. It was a buzzing sound followed by the faint slap of leaves rustling as if in a breeze. Then the rifle fire thundered up the valley and made the birds shriek as they flapped free of the tall trees.

A cacophony of gunfire erupted again, somewhat closer, but from a different direction. Lacroix was puzzled but Knight knew instantly what was happening.

'They set up lines of riflemen at different points and at different distances. They're firing at separate points on the trail or in the tree-line with the hope of flushing me out. It's a gamble.'

'That's a waste of ammunition.'

'Sure, but after last night they know I'm watching so they're assuming I'm nearby. If they're lucky I'll be close enough to feel the sting of their lead.'

'But you're not,' Lacroix said smiling, 'you're sitting here with a belly full of turkey and a bottle of whiskey.' Lacroix's glee was palpable.

'True enough, but my friends down there won't give up. I've got to figure out a way to end this.'

'That's a fact. Now let me ponder on this a moment.' Lacroix put the bottle to his lips and took a long draw, and smacked his lips appreciatively before corking the bottle. 'Now the way I see it we have to come at them from two sides and fight like General Washington's boys, picking away at them a little each day.'

'We?'

'Of course, you dang fool. I'm in this now, too. Fact is, I haven't had this much fun since my wife showed me the Injun fertility ritual of dancing naked under a full moon!'

'Is that right? Did it work?'

'Hell, no, but I sure enjoyed it all the same.' Lacroix's laughter echoed in the cave.

Late in the afternoon they decided to chance looking around. Knight figured they had about two hours of daylight left. Down on the switchback trail they moved north and followed the same trail as the night before. 'Let's head for that mountain creek,' Lacroix said. 'I got a feeling it isn't too safe down near the lake right now.'

Up in the hills they were forced to break through a thick covering of bushes and small trees to reach the creek. The creek itself at this point wasn't twenty feet across, but deep, the water dark and green and shaded on each side by underbrush and squat fat bushes. Lacroix said he had another canoe stowed somewhere nearby but couldn't quite remember where it was. They found it after thirty minutes of scampering along the hidden embankment. The small bark canoe was stuck in a bush of raspberries. Knight saw a grizzly paw print in the mud. He pointed it out to Lacroix.

'We can't stay long here. That grizzly has been hunting around these parts all summer. The black bears I don't mind, but a grizzly will hunt a man down.'

'Does this creek feed into the lake?'

'That it does. There's lots of turns and some shallows. It bottoms out in a marsh about forty feet from my other canoe. There's a paddle under that rawhide cover. Keep it in mind if you need to get away fast. Now let's mosey south toward the lake on foot. This brush makes good cover.'

'As long as we don't meet that grizzly,' Knight said.

Lacroix patted his flintlock rifle affectionately. 'That's why I brought this along, and you've got that fancy Winchester.'

'We're an industrious pair.'

They moved slowly along a trail of their own making, although Knight relied on Lacroix to navigate. The old mountain man appeared to know every nook and cranny of this section of the Rocky Mountains. As they came closer to the lake they heard distant voices. Emerging from the thick underbrush, they eventually crouched low and watched for trouble. They had not seen any other men nor heard any voices, but Knight's skin was prickling along his neck as his instincts warned him of danger.

Judging it safe, they pressed ahead and continued toward the lake's southern ridge. They had not gone fifty feet when five men appeared suddenly on the forest path in front of them. The men, startled by the sudden appearance of two armed men, went for the guns. One man, raising his rifle swiftly, managed to fire once. The bullet whizzed past Knight's ear. Lacroix's flintlock boomed and a lead ball shattered the man's head. Knight dove to his right, levering his Winchester. A bullet tore a hole through a man's leg. The man screamed, raising his revolver and snapped two shots in Knight's direction. Rolling into the brush, Knight sent a shot at the man but missed. All of the men had fired at least once and scattered. The quick, lethal burst of gunfire echoed throughout the forest.

With his knee caroming off a rock, Knight winced in pain and scrambled deeper into the underbrush. He heard the sound of Lacroix's Navy Colt boom once followed by the sound of the old mountain man chuckling happily. *The old coot is enjoying himself*, Knight thought.

They had one wounded man and three armed men to deal with. Worst of all, the gunfire would bring more men. They didn't have much time. Knight crept about a line of blackberry bushes. He wanted to move closer to the men. He thumbed a few fresh cartridges into his Winchester to replace the ones he'd used. With a full magazine and Lacroix taking shots with his old Navy revolver, Knight thought they'd be able to handle these men as long as they did so quickly.

Peeking out from a cluster of leaves, Knight sighted down his Winchester on one of the men. He fired without hesitation. The Winchester barked and its bullet found its mark on the man's chest. Knight watched the man gawk at his wound, crimson blossoming on his plaid shirt, and then fall unceremoniously into a thicket.

Three to go.

He kept moving, feeling neither fear nor elation; his mind was simply focused on doing the job at hand. When he saw a shape emerge from a thicket he fired, the gunshot echoing loudly and scattering more birds. Then he was moving again. He thought his shot might have missed but at that moment it didn't matter. More shapes in a swelter of rippling leaves – he fired again. He could hear nothing but the echo of his rifle. A few moments later he spotted droplets of blood on some tufts of grass. So he had at least wounded one of them.

The embankment dropped away and he almost stumbled. A gun roared and a bullet nicked his left arm. Pain lanced his arm but he still pressed on.

He heard voices. A man cursed.

Wheeling around he saw a man about to raise his

revolver and he dropped to his knees, jacked a round into his Winchester, and fired. Flame blew out of the muzzle. His bullet cut the air before thunking into the man's jaw, a geyser of blood and bone spilling across the trail.

Knight moved past the twitching body.

Two to go.

Lacroix's revolver popped some distance off on his left. He moved in that direction. Far removed from their original path, Knight was nearly crashing through the underbrush with brute force. His exertions caused his energy to ebb, his breath finally coming in rasping gulps. *Hell of a thing getting old*, he thought as he crashed through a web of chokecherry scrub.

He stopped, squinting through the scrub. A man a hundred yards away facing east. He had a rifle and he was looking about, half crouched by a moss-covered boulder. Knight pulled his Winchester to his shoulder and sighted down the barrel. He heard a bluejay singing when he pulled the trigger just once. He saw flame spew from the rifle's maw and singe a branch as the bullet sped toward the man a hundred yards away. The bluejay tweeted once, hurriedly, perhaps startled by the rifle shot.

He saw a puff of dust rise off the man's vest. The man dropped his rifle.

Knight leapt to his feet, cursing his own tired bones. It took him longer than he intended to reach the man. Knight stood a few feet away and studied him. He was still breathing. He looked like any down-on-his luck cowboy. The sun poured down through the spruce and appeared to circle the man with a golden glow. He looked up and saw Knight.

'You the marshal?'

Knight nodded. 'Why are you after me?'

The man chuckled but then coughed up blood. 'You got me, mister, that's a fact. Do you have a canteen?'

'No.'

'Too bad. I would have liked a cool drink.'

'Are you going to tell me what this is all about?'

'Money. Manchester pays in gold.'

'Why me?'

'You killed his brother.'

'I've never heard of any Manchester.'

The man shrugged, coughed, blood trickling from his nose.

'Lousy goddamn luck. I have a whore girlfriend in Denver. Not even enough time to writer her a letter.'

'Don't worry about her. She won't be lonely.'

'That's downright cruel of you to say so.'

'Being a lawman isn't a friendly business.'

'Manchester has fifty men. You don't have a chance. I hope you suffer when he kills you.'

'Sure,' Knight said, but the man was dead. His body relaxed slowly as he toppled over. Knight looked up at the sun blazing in the blue bowl of sky. He looked up and down the trail. The birds had started tweeting again. You wouldn't know that four men had just been shot to death. Nature didn't care. It was a beautiful day.

One to go.

Thirty minutes later, Knight had moved along a deer trail and circled around looking for Lacroix. He found the mountain man sitting on a log and casually swatting away some black flies that were hovering around his beard. Perspiration shone on his face.

'I took some shots at a few,' Lacroix said, 'and I might have winged one.'

'I killed four.'

Lacroix gestured to his left. 'One vamoosed up thataway. Might have hit him, like I said. I'll rest here a spell, but don't take too long. I'm expecting company.'

'We're too far away from the cave to get caught out here.'

Lacroix smiled. 'I have more than one camp. Now get moving.'

Knight went after his man. Under any other circumstance he might have paused and enjoyed the beautiful Colorado weather as the sun shined down among the pines. Then he saw a speck of blood on a pine cone at his feet. The wounded man had come this way. Knight checked his guns, re-loaded, and jacked a round into his '73 Winchester. Moving into the brush he crested a hill and stared down a sloping, broad trail that dropped off suddenly into a ravine. Down in that ravine he saw the man slip into a strangle-hold of scrub and small trees. The man had boxed himself in, but that didn't make him any less dangerous.

The breeze scuttled along and threw windblown grit in his face. He could smell the pine as two pheasants burst from the scrub down in the ravine and flapped away. Knight thought the man was either a damn fool or his wound was such that he couldn't think clearly. He lost direct sight of the man but the branches were wavering where Knight had last seen him.

A rifle thundered.

Knight felt the bullet cut the air just an inch from his head, followed by another shot. By then he was dodging low, winging off a shot of his own down into that scrub. The distance was about two hundred yards and without getting the man centered in his buckhorn sights he didn't much think he'd hit anything.

Knight didn't want to spend the time playing a cat and mouse game with a wounded man. Besides, the outcome was inevitable. Crouching on a hillock, he removed his Stetson and whipped it into the air while shouldering his rifle, quickly levering a round into the breech, and focusing on the brush where the man was hiding. He saw the muzzle flash as the blue smoke wafted upwards.

Knight fired at the spot, his rifle booming, and then he emptied his Winchester by firing in a sweeping motion left and right to cover the entire area. He reloaded his Winchester before starting down the hill. He knew the man was dead. He heard his bullet strike bone and the man's gurgling death rattle even though he couldn't see him.

He found the body lying face-up in a cluster of yellow wild-flowers. Knight recognized him. It was the young kid he'd clubbed that night this all started. Now he was dead. Hell, it had been damn foolish to let him live anyway. *These men won't hesitate to kill me if they get a chance*, he thought.

What he really wanted were answers, but in order to understand all of this he needed to get to Silas Manchester, whoever he was. Meanwhile, Maxfield Knight had no choice. He was going to have to kill a lot of men before this was over.

Forty-five to go.

SIX

Cole Tibbs thought that US Marshal Knight had his hands full with fifty armed men after him. He sat astride his horse up on a hill thick with spruce and birch and watched the camp. They had tents set up as if it were a military operation, a cook wagon and sentries. They were well armed and well fed. Not to mention, they could hunt game here in the mountains for extra food. The sons-of-bitches meant business. Now Tibbs had to come up with a plan to help.

His first thought was to remove his deputy US Marshal's star and ride into camp pretending to be a drifting gun for hire. In that manner he might assist Max when they caught up with him, and with this many men Tibbs thought it was a sure thing they'd catch up with the marshal. Knight wouldn't run. Problem was, some of these men might know him from town and if they had seen him with the marshal he wouldn't have a chance. So he decided to remain in hiding and watch and learn. He might see something that could be useful, and if the opportunity presented itself he might even be able to whittle the odds down in the marshal's favor. But he had to be careful.

He spent the night in a strand of pines. The trees here

were thick, growing so closely together that the lower branches were bare and the uppermost section of the pines spread out like a canopy of pine needles. The ground was littered with pine cones and would have been ideal for a fire-pit, but Tibbs decided against it. Making a fire could draw attention his way, and he didn't want that. Besides, he had been eating well on his fishing trip and didn't mind the hard jerky he chewed on. He would have Knight buy him a nice steak dinner once he got him out of this mess.

The men in the camp were organized. They rode out in increments of six and returned no fewer than four hours later. A rotating squad of six men, all searching for the marshal. On the first day he heard gunfire in the distant hills, but there was no indication they had found Max.

Tibbs concentrated on identifying their leader. It didn't take him long to see the large, bald man with the handlebar moustache coming and going from his tent. The man was enormous, at least six feet five inches and more than three hundred pounds. His bald head gleamed with perspiration. His wide shoulders and fat body gave him an unreal appearance. His manner and bearing reminded Tibbs of a snake-oil salesman – all dramatic gestures and loud commands but amounting to nothing. Still, he looked formidable. He wore an ivory-handled Colt. His vest had gold buttons. His pants looked to be of the finest material. He barked orders like a sergeant. A real pompous son of a bitch.

Tibbs watched carefully to see who might rate as second-in-command, but he was lacking in candidates. All the other men appeared to be hired help. There was no hierarchy or chain of command that Tibbs could see. That was unusual. Tibbs decided he had made the right choice by laying low.

His aim was to find Max and help get him away from these men as fast as possible. Tibbs was hidden up in the hills east of the camp, meaning that Max was holed up somewhere in the western foothills of the Rockies. Max would fight, and Tibbs had no doubt that a great many of these men would die before they gunned the marshal down. Tibbs would wage a one-man war from the opposite side, hopefully confusing these men.

That afternoon they brought Max's horse into camp. He watched the men carefully as they examined the horse. The saddlebags, bedroll and Winchester were missing. So Max had some food supplies and ammunition. Tibbs knew the marshal was a capable outdoorsman and would easily hunt rabbits and squirrels to feed himself. The big man that Tibbs was certain was Silas Manchester showed no outward signs of emotion. He looked over the horse, said something to his men, and returned to his tent.

They had the horses picketed on the eastern side of camp, closest to Tibbs. Those horses presented Tibbs his first opportunity to cause some confusion, but first he needed a place to hide because they would certainly search these hills afterward. Even as a plan formed in his mind, Tibbs had another thought that made more sense. He sat quietly for several hours simply observing the camp and noted several crucial details. They had guards near the horses only on the interior, close to the first line of tents. No guards scouted the perimeter. That was certainly a flaw in their thinking.

The horses were actually picketed in three sections. They'd cut down young but long pines and created three squared-off corrals over a flat section of prairie grass. They made a water trough for each section. The first two sections were side by side and connected by a makeshift interior gate. The third section was independent of the others and on the eastern edge of camp. Knight's horse had gone in here. The saddles were arranged haphazardly, draped over the topmost lodge pole. The saddles added to the illusion of a barrier. Although this was all a makeshift construction, it was effective as long as they kept an eye on the horses.

If Tibbs was going to attack in hit-and-run maneuvers he would need to be on foot. His horse would be too easy to track. Knight had already obviously come to that conclusion. While Tibbs had initially thought to let the horses loose, or at least some of them, he now revised his plan. A solitary man stood a better chance of staying alive by hiding from pursuit, and the Rocky Mountains offered endless sanctuaries for a determined man. He examined the tall trees where he was camped and made a note of the thick pine needle canopy.

Once he made up his mind it was a matter of waiting. Tibbs had learned from Maxfield Knight in just of a few short years of riding with him that being fast with a gun wasn't enough to keep any lawman alive. You had to develop an instinct for circumstances, and react accordingly. He waited until the stars were shimmering in the lavender sky and the tall grass was swaying gently in the warm night wind. He watched three elk emerge from the trees north of the camp and stand chewing at the sage and brush, their ears flicking nervously when they heard any loud voice from the camp.

They had several campfires going, and the men in camp seemed disciplined, and perhaps even a little bored. Surprisingly, there was no sign of alcohol. Only a great deal of money could have made such a scene a reality, for these were all hardened gunmen or cowhands desperate for money yet still accustomed to a saloon's pleasures. They talked and smoked, and drank coffee and told bawdy stories.

The glittering stars had begun to crawl across the horizon when Tibbs led his horse out of the trees and began his long walk down the foothills toward camp. He took his time, holding the horse's reins, walking casually and calmly out of the trees and across that long plain of whispering grass. The night was warm, the air languid. In another time and place he might enjoy such a walk with his girl, Jamie, at his side, but such moments would have to wait. The tall grass was swaying back and forth as they cut a path through the cattails and wildflowers.

He came up to the corral an hour after beginning his walk. After unsaddling his horse, he lifted the pole and allowed his horse to trot into the corral. Eventually, he would find Knight's horse for the two had ridden together often. Tibbs draped his saddle over the crude fence line and immediately turned his back on the corral and walked away. The sun would be up in but a short time, but the camp was quiet.

This was the most dangerous time in his plan. He had waited most of the night before putting his plan in motion. If anyone should notice him he'd be in trouble. A moment passed where the skin was prickling on the back of his neck, but the night remained quiet. It was a gamble, but he didn't think anyone would notice the extra horse and saddle. There were simply too many horses, and these men were careless about the horses.

When he was halfway into the tall grass he slipped to his knees to make himself invisible. He had taken enough chances, but the gamble had paid off – so far. Moving out of the tall grass a few minutes later placed him near a line of thin birch trees. Tibbs had just moved near the trees when a horse nickered and twigs snapped beneath a shod hoof. Immediately crouching low, he peered around to locate the rider.

The man on horseback was thirty feet away, the glow of his cigarette illuminating his scraggly features. The man was parallel with Tibbs, his face a golden silhouette as he sucked on his tobacco.

Of all the damn bad luck. He had come this far only to nearly blunder into a late-night sentry. Then the man's horse flicked its ears and turned its neck to stare at Tibbs. The man turned his head, following the horse's gaze. Tibbs couldn't take any chances. He was close enough to be seen, even if the man was half blind. Tibbs leapt forward, his legs pumping as he ran directly at the man. He had his hands on the man's legs and began yanking him from the saddle just as the cowboy realized what was happening and tried to pull his gun.

Tibbs slammed his knuckled fist into the man's nose as he slid forward, but Tibbs was off balance and together they fell in a heap. A knee came up and grazed his ribcage. Tibbs retaliated mercilessly, pummeling the man with his fists as quickly as he could send his knuckles hammering at the man's head. The man was tough – tougher than Tibbs had expected. More damn bad luck.

A fist raked Tibbs, his jaw bruised. The man sprang to his feet and unleashed his own blistering flurry of punches. Once, twice, three times and Tibbs felt a tooth come loose with the last punch. He spat blood.

A solid jaw, breaking punch knocked Tibbs to his knees. Rather than give up, however, Tibbs pushed himself head first into the man hoping to buy some time and shake the cobwebs loose from his head. They grappled and Tibbs kicked the man mercilessly in the right thigh. Tibbs knew well that such a kick would do painful damage to the leg's muscle, especially when the kick was delivered by the toe of a new pair of rawhide boots.

'Aaah! Damn you!' the man howled.

Ignoring his pounding head and his own pain, Tibbs kicked the man viciously between the legs. Doubling over in pain, the man grunted in agony, clutching at his crotch. Tibbs landed a haymaker right next to his left eye, his knuckles cracking the cheekbone. The man flopped forward and vomited into the grass.

Ignoring the stench, Tibbs leaped on to his back and hooked his arms around the man's neck. The smell was horrendous, a combination of blood and vomit, but Tibbs knew he had to finish the fight quickly.

He began choking the man. His muscles tensed, his fist tightened, his other arm across the back of the man's neck while his right arm crushed his Adam's apple. Thrashing wildly then, the man nearly broke free by lurching forward, but Tibbs held him fast. Squeezing tightly, unrelenting, showing no mercy, Tibbs heard the man choking, his tongue lolling from between his lips. He squeezed harder.

Fingers clawed at Tibbs, legs jerked spasmodically. He squeezed harder.

The gasping and gurgling sounds were horrific and not something that Tibbs would easily forget, but he had no choice. He exerted more pressure. Slowly the man's efforts to break free were diminished, but still Tibbs squeezed.

When at last the body was still he slowly released his hold, sweat dripping from his forehead, his arms aching from his tremendous effort. He rose slowly and looked around. The man's horse had run off. He stepped away from the corpse and forced in a lungful of air to clear his head. Without thinking, his right hand slapped at his holster to check his gun. He still had it.

He figured the horse would head toward the corral where it knew it would find food, and since the corral wasn't all that far away Tibbs now faced limited options. They would come looking for the dead man they would find here in the tall grass. *Nothing wrong with that,* Tibbs thought, *except he hadn't come up with a hiding place yet.* But a thought struck him, wild though it was.

The sky had paled as the sun rose. The stars were fading. He had to move fast. He heard the wind strum the grass and ruffle the leaves of those tall oaks; and then he was sprinting up a slope and into the sanctuary of the hills.

The shadows were cool beneath the trees and the scent of pine brushed away the lingering scent of death that clung to him after strangling the man in the meadow. Looking up, he studied several pines that grew close together. The lower branches were bereft of leaves because no sun touched this area; the trees were so tall that only the uppermost branches flourished with pine needles.

Climbing the tree was easy. He went carefully, his boot pushing off branches, careful not to break any and leave a sign. When he was above the blanket of pine needles he surveyed his surroundings and decided he could hide his bedroll up there. Climbing down again, he retrieved his bedroll, which had extra cartridges wrapped in the blankets and some modest food stuff such as dried beef and a few biscuits. Tibbs climbed up and fixed his bedroll in the branches by tying the bundle to a branch with a leather cord. When he climbed down and walked about the base of the tree and examined the view from different angles, his bedroll couldn't be seen.

The high grass was changing color with the movement of the sun, drenched in gold and then muted as a cloud passed overhead. Looking out across the plain, he saw activity in the camp. He assumed they had found the body.

He went back into the trees, into the shadiest section far off any animal trail, where the sun glanced off the pine blankets and where the trees grew so close together the upper branches sheltered the forest bed from the sun. He looked up. He would have his rifle with him and he couldn't drop it. The Colt revolver would have minimal effectiveness if they saw him.

If they saw him.

Tibbs had to make certain they didn't see him, or find any sign of him.

Criss-crossing the area, he left scuff marks among the fallen branches and needled bed, leading them in circles, until finally he wandered off and down into the grass. Then back into the pines walking backward. The trick would confuse any skilled hunter. Knight, he realized, would face the same problem. The fact that Knight was still alive meant that either these men weren't all that skilled at tracking, or Knight was simply the better man. Tibbs, believed – hoped – that a little of both were true.

He waited an hour watching the camp when he saw the

riders coming. He took his time, careful where he stepped, and, when he was again sheltered from the rapidly rising sun, he picked his tree, eyed the swaying blanket of pines above him, and began climbing.

SEVEN

Silas Manchester lay on the cot in his tent and fell asleep watching the shadows scamper across the tent flaps as the sun beat down. His breakfast of eggs and venison had made him tired. With a full belly he was inclined to rest awhile, content that his gold had bought him men that would help him avenge his brother's death.

He dreamed fitfully, his pulse hammering in his temples. His mind conjured images of a night years back in a Savannah whorehouse where the bitch, Lucy, had become drunk and tried to claw his eyes out. He recalled the yellow flames of the oil lamps in the room, and the swaying shadows that danced across the wall. Downstairs, the piano player hit a wrong key and he heard the squeal of laughter. Whores were easily amused.

When Lucy had come lurching at him he backhanded her with such force that her eyes rolled white in their sockets as she fell back. Within minutes her face had swollen. When she regained consciousness she apologized, no doubt fearful that he would harm her further. Little did she know that Silas Manchester was the type of man that liked to hire other men to do his bidding for him.

So a week later he paid a man to kill Lucy. Then he paid another man to kill that man. Silas Manchester talked with gold, believed in the power of gold and silver, and used gold as the ultimate weapon. The gold never failed him. Men were weak, foolish, lacking in ambition, but with gold they rose to any occasion dictated by Manchester.

Gold would bring down Maxfield Knight.

Lying in his tent he dreamed the grinning skull that visited him each night in his mind was that of the soon to be deceased US marshal. He dreamed a landscape of grinning skulls falling from the heavens and rolling at his feet, their gold teeth clattering as the skulls laughed.

He awoke with a dry mouth.

The nightmares had been getting worse. There was a nagging thought in the back of his mind that he had somehow made a mistake. But what was it? He had no idea. Certainly, Knight was formidable. He had already eluded fifty men, a remarkable fact considering that Knight was alone. And the fact that Knight was alone was something of which Manchester was absolutely certain. His men had watched him in the town of Cherrywood Crossing, and other than the sheriff, Knight had kept to himself.

But something wasn't right.

He pulled himself from his cot, poured a glass of Kentucky whiskey and splashed it down his throat.

It was those damn arrows that had killed a few of his men. Arrows.

There might be some old Indians living in the mountains, but attacking a force of well-armed white men made no sense. The Apache wars were ending and this far north the Indians avoided white men. The Sioux were docile these days.

Manchester had instructed his men to bring him the arrows so that he might examine them himself. He had two arrows lying on his table next to his oil lamp. They were well made, with goosefeathers and forged from stone. He wasn't an expert on arrows, but they looked authentic enough. Still, he never believed for a moment that an Indian had attacked his men. Nor did he believe that Maxfield Knight had used these arrows. So there had to be another player in the game. Manchester didn't like that at all.

He went outside his tent and gestured for the closest man to come over.

'What's your name?' Manchester barked.

'Larry.'

Okay, Larry, ask around camp for the best tracker. Ask some of those half-breeds and Mexicans. Tell them if they say they're good trackers they can prove it and get a bonus. I have something special for them to do.'

'Sure boss.'

As the man went away Manchester saw a commotion over near the corral. Irritated, he strode toward the corral where several men were bringing a body into camp. When they saw Manchester approaching they stopped.

'What the hell happened?'

'This is Paul,' one of the men said. 'He was on guard duty and I found him out there.' The man gestured past the corral at the long field.

'Damn it!' Manchester spat the words. 'Take him away and bury him. Keep his guns and his gold. Then get ten men and go up into those hills and look around. Most likely you won't find anyone, but if you do, kill them.'

Fifty gunmen paid with gold and five or six were dead

already. It was preposterous. Manchester looked up at the tall pines on the hills. If Knight had made his way around and was now hiding on the opposite side of their camp then he was far better than anyone might have imagined, but Manchester didn't believe that. No, there were other players here, and that sobering fact made him all the angrier.

They would all die. Whoever they were, no matter their motivation, Manchester would see the vultures pick the flesh from their bones.

Returning to his tent, he strapped on his gunbelt. He wasn't afraid, but neither was he foolish. The hunt had changed somehow, and until he learned more he would be cautious. He went out again and stood watching the camp. A few men glanced up at him when he emerged. They were watching to see if he gave anyone orders, but Manchester simply stood there quietly looking around.

Was Knight hiding in plain view right here in camp? Or did he have any conspirators working on his behalf and unknown to them?

Strolling the camp, he smoked a thin cigar and greeted the men, sometimes giving them orders. He was a large man, beefy with broad shoulders, his eyes dark and without emotion. Although he was overweight, Manchester was strong, and he had made a point of demonstrating how strong when he consented to a hand-wrestling contest on their first day in camp. Winning easily, he knew the man's hand was fractured, although he wisely hadn't complained about it.

Having already established a routine of patrols, he was satisfied that his men were doing everything possible to locate the elusive marshal. He had an outlying camp near the swamp that had proven fatal to a few men, so he added fifteen men to the outlying post. A patrol of twelve men were already in the hills, both on horseback and on foot. The patrol he'd added to reconnoitre the eastern hills left just over a dozen men in camp.

Hell, I might have hired a hundred men to track this bastard down, he thought.

He stopped by the cook's wagon and spoke with Juan, the old Mexican cook who claimed he once made a beef stew for old Andrew Jackson. Manchester liked the biscuits and Juan assured him he had enough flour and supplies to feed everyone for another week. Manchester grunted his satisfaction and strode away.

He sat outside his tent with a small folding table on which he placed the whiskey bottle and a small glass. He finished his cigar and sipped his whiskey.

He thought about his childhood in Atlanta and his half-brother, Diego, the son of his father's maid, Manita. Manchester never knew his own mother as she died the day of his birth. His father, however, lived a long life and died but recently, but not before instructing his son to avenge his brother's death.

'Diego was but a cur, a spawn of that whore maid who served no purpose other than satisfying a man's lust. But he was still blood. He got what he deserved when that lawman beat him to death, but he was still blood. Do you understand?'

'I understand.'

'Do you remember that first hunting trip we took to Africa? Do you recall, Silas, the thrill we experienced when we tracked those lions into the brush? Do you recall the hot sun and sweat

on your brow as your finger curled on the trigger? One false move and one of us or both of us might have died. Now I am telling you this because to hunt a man, a rational and calculating man, is far more dangerous than hunting the lions of Africa. Killing a man is nothing if it's unexpected. Give this lawman a chance, enjoy the challenge of the hunt, and kill him in the name of your brother, that worthless cur, Diego.'

His father's watery eyes were bloodshot, his skin wrinkled like the old Zulu warriors they had met on the Dark Continent; and when he spoke a line of drool spotted his chin. Manchester felt little love for the old man, but he did respect him. The old man had made a fortune, and Silas Manchester was eager to bury his father because he would inherit a fortune to rival John Jacob Astor's.

After his second shot of whiskey, with his throat still warm from the alcohol, a notion struck Manchester, so he fetched his writing utensils and drafted a short letter. Manchester was a man of few words. He lived by the principle that his actions spoke for him, and that gold bought him loyalty. When the letter was finished he folded it, slipping it into his vest pocket.

Then he read for a while, enjoying the sunlight on his gleaming, bald head. He had *Harper's Magazine*, and several New York newspapers that he'd brought for just such a relaxing moment.

Two things happened an hour later that would shape his destiny, and it's to his credit that he recognized their importance although he had no way of guessing the outcome.

A man approached. He was small, dusty, dark-skinned, and Manchester correctly guessed he was a half-breed.

'Boss, I heard you need a tracker,' the man said.

'I do, and what is your name?'

'Castellanos.'

'Do you have a first name Castellanos?'

'Ramone, boss, my name is Ramone, but they've always just called me Castellanos.'

'Are you a half-breed?'

Manchester studied the man's eyes. He was pleased there was no sign of him being offended by the question. The man never blinked. His face was a mask. Castellanos nodded. 'My mother was an Italian and my father was from Spain. I think that makes me a half-breed.'

'Interesting mixture. I would have guessed Mexican and Negro. How well can you track?'

'As well as any man, boss.'

'I'll give you a chance to prove it. I believe the man we are hunting isn't alone. I don't know how that happened, but it has. I want you to pinpoint where they are. There must be some camp, or some way they are staying hidden. Maybe a cave. Find them, and come back to tell me. When you learn something, anything at all, you come back and report it. I want you to report it even if it's not specific; even if it's simply a general area. I want something – anything, and then I'll attack. Do you understand?'

Castellanos nodded. 'Yes, I understand.' He turned and gestured at the mountains. 'I have an idea already. I've been thinking about what has happened. Those are not an Indian's arrows.'

'I'm impressed. Yes, that's right. He has an ally, and that explains the arrows.'

'Some of the men are good trackers, but they can't think

like I can. I can see when I hunt, the way an animal sees, and I can plan.'

'Good. Those are precisely the qualities I'm looking for.' Manchester took the letter from his pocket and gave it to Castellanos. 'If the opportunity presents itself then give this letter to the man we hunt, the marshal. Give it to no other but Maxfield Knight. See to it that you don't get killed doing it, because I would enjoy knowing that he's read this letter.'

Castellanos nodded. 'I'll do it.'

Manchester dismissed Castellanos with a wave of his hand. The wiry half-breed vanished like a shadow finding shade. Manchester was satisfied. Gold had bought him some good men after all, and he had no doubt that Castellanos would find the marshal.

The second moment of importance occurred when Silas Manchester sat outside his tent and enjoyed his whiskey. He watched the horses in the corral for a long while. He could see them well enough even from a sitting position, and he admired their strength and independence. Soon thereafter his men returned from scouring the pine-studded hills. He waited patiently as they dismounted and walked their horses to the corral. Finally, they approached him. The man he knew was named Joe removed his Stetson and wiped the sweat from his face.

'Boss, we looked all over those hills but we didn't find anyone. There's horse tracks and boot prints all over the place, so we know someone was there. It was hard to read the signs. Could be anyone was roamin' about in those hills.'

'As I expected,' Manchester said. 'Anyone can be anyone, sort of like a riddle isn't it?'

'What's that, boss?'

'Never mind. I've been sitting here and enjoying my whiskey, and as I was looking out at the corral I noticed a horse I hadn't seen before. Have you brought in any strays other than the marshal's horse?'

'No, boss, I don't know anything about any extra horses.'

'Get yourselves some grub. No harm done.'

Men, horses and gold were the three things that Silas Manchester understood better than anything, and in that instant when he noticed the fine stallion that lingered near the marshal's horse, he knew with great certainty that some prophecy was being fulfilled; some ancient destiny of death was about to play out here in the mountains, and he was as determined as ever to honor his father's wishes and do right by his brother, no matter what trickery his enemies used to befuddle him. After all, blood was blood.

EIGHT

It was mid-morning of a summer's day and if they had not known better the two men might have believed this was Eden before the Fall and no serpents threatened them. But Lacroix and Knight were well aware of the force of armed men that hunted them; and so a summer's day might prove beautiful to the eyes, not unlike a woman, but possessing an edge like a knife that cut very deep.

'I used lodgepole pine,' Lacroix was explaining, 'and built a shelter I could crawl into if I got caught in a storm. You see, I've a hankerin' to fish, and when I fish I lose all track of time.'

'I have a friend with the same habit. I'm hoping you get to meet him soon.'

Lacroix squinted at Knight. 'Is that so? Well, anyway, I cut these poles and made this shelter. It's simple enough, and it keeps the rain off a man.'

'You made it far enough from the trail, but this is hardly a good hiding place.'

'It's not a hiding place at all, just a shelter from storms.'

The shelter was about seven feet long and four feet high, set back in the brush and invisible to anyone passing. There was just enough room for a man to crawl in and sleep off a storm. The covering was all leaves and mud, layered so that the shelter wouldn't leak.

'I've slept here when I'm out fishing,' Lacroix said. 'I have to shag out the snakes and raccoons, and it's right comfortable when you get used to it.'

'What about the other hiding place you mentioned?'

'That's just up the trail a way.'

'Hell,' Knight growled, 'It's a nice day for a walk.'

Lacroix grinned. Soon, they passed the bark canoe near the creek where they'd hidden it again, but this time they continued north in a straight line. They were several miles now from Lacroix's cave dwelling.

When they emerged from a strand of birch trees after following a meandering deer trail and saw the four wolves watching them up the trail, Knight had a sinking feeling that their luck had changed for the worse. The four wolves were lined up in a row not two hundred yards away, and they didn't look scared.

'Well, I'll be,' Lacroix said.

'I saw their tracks a few days ago. Lots of grizzly tracks, too.'

'I don't know which I like less, the wolves or the grizzly. I will say that a grizzly pelt brings me more money, not to mention that it keeps me warm in winter.'

'I suggest we turn around.'

Lacroix shook his head. 'No sir, that won't help. They're hungry. Look at their eyes.'

Knight saw it all right; hunger looked the same in any living creature's eyes, and it wasn't pleasant.

'They'll hunt us now,' Lacroix continued, 'so I reckon we

best get to killing them as fast as we can.'

'That'll sure let everyone know where we are.'

'That it will. The one on the far left is mine.'

In an instant, Lacroix threw his rifle to his shoulder, squinted down the barrel and stabbed a shot at the wolf. The slug found its mark and shattered the wolf's skull. Knight, having no time to admire Lacroix's marksmanship, levered from the hip, firing on instinct, his bullets whamming into fur and bone as the wolves attacked. In the next moment the air was a blur of snarling fangs and deep yellow eyes alight with hunger. A wolf fell at Knight's boots, its head torn apart, the legs kicking spasmodically. There was no time to breathe.

Lacroix, having spent the solitary slug in his flintlock rifle, pulled his 1851 Navy Colt and fired as another wolf lunged. The wolf fell dead just inches from his feet. Knight swung his rifle around and blasted the last wolf seconds before its fangs would have torn apart Lacroix's leg.

The echo of gunfire bounded through the trees as the gunsmoke drifted in the air around them.

'Reload,' Knight said.

Lacroix didn't need to be told twice. He reloaded his colt first and then his flintlock. Knight reloaded his Winchester.

'How much time do you figure we have?'

'Depends on how far away they are,' Lacroix said. 'I suppose they could be on us quick enough, and there's still a way to go before we get to where we need to be.' Lacroix eyed the four dead wolves sadly. 'It's a shame to leave these pelts but we don't have time for skinning.'

The sky seemed to open up and unleash showers of sunlight. In the stillness, the air was hot. This time, Lacroix was sweating. He unbuttoned his buckskin shirt to let the air get at his skin. They trudged along, much slower than either of them wished, besieged by birdcalls, the sent of fresh pine on a mid-summer's afternoon, and assailed by the notion that death was galloping in their direction.

It wasn't long before the skin was prickling on the back of Knight's neck as they cut along a deer path and started to ascend a hill thick with sapling and scrub. Once over the hill, they moved rather quickly through a long gully before ascending another hill and edging up into a rocky formation that towered above them like the parapets of an ancient castle.

'Home away from home,' Lacroix said. 'We need to be careful not to leave any sign. No boot marks or broken twigs. And this is going to be difficult, but judging by the commotion I hear behind us, we don't have any choice.'

'Lead on.'

Knight was irritated. He hadn't wanted to get caught out in the middle of nowhere, but the wolf-pack attack had left them little choice. And Lacroix was right; the sound of neighing horses and disgruntled men was louder. They were being hunted again, and this time by a larger force.

The wild country was spread out on either side; the valleys and forest, deep crags and towering cliffs all made their trek a dangerous venture. The Rocky Mountains were uncaring; a force of nature that extinguished life with the blink of an eye. A storm, a misstep, or encounters with a wild beast were all enough to test the average man's mettle. For miles uncounted on either side of them the valleys and trees seemed impenetrable, and the mountains themselves a barrier that appeared capable of crushing them with landslides or other treacheries of the lone trail.

Death nipped at their heels.

When they paused to rest and drink some water from Lacroix's canteen, Knight offered a suggestion that they stand and fight, but Lacroix didn't agree. He stated that, might they succeed in hiding, it would confuse their pursuers all the more. Fear, he said, was a weapon they should exploit. Knight thought it over and agreed grudgingly.

It took the better part of the day to reach Lacroix's second hideaway. It was another cave, but this one at ground level, accessible by squeezing into a rocky crevice where once a great storm of creation cut the rock with centuries of rain and ice. Thirty feet along this thin split in the mountain they found a cave entrance. As Knight expected, the entrance was hidden by a barrier of branches lashed together and made to look like natural tumbleweed.

'I'm getting too fat for this,' Lacroix grumbled, 'but we have to crouch low and crawl in. I'll go first and get a lamp lit. You pull those branches back to cover the hole.'

Lacroix was holding an oil lamp high when Knight crawled inside and lumbered to his feet. Every muscle in his body ached from their day-long walk.

The cave was sparsely furnished, nowhere near the comfortable environment that Lacroix had created with his primary residence. A circle of stones marked the fire pit, still loaded with twigs and branches for Lacroix was a man that thought ahead. There was the oil lamp and a tin of extra oil. Lacroix had matchsticks in his pocket.

'This place is what I call "just in case" if you know what I mean.'

'I get the idea.'

'As I get older and fatter I don't reckon I'll be able to climb that cliff back home, so when the day comes I'll move here.'

'It's a good idea to have a plan.'

'I know some better caves, but further north. This one is about like the others. Speaking of plans, I reckon we better come up with one.'

'I was thinking the same thing,' Knight agreed, 'I thought come sundown I'd go out and stir up trouble. I can spend a night in that shelter you showed me.'

Lacroix nodded. 'I'll go back and see what the trail looks like. If an opportunity presents itself I'll stir up some trouble, too.' Lacroix grinned and winked at Knight. 'Maybe we can whittle them down one by one.'

'Maybe,' Knight said, 'but I don't plan on being here come Christmas.'

He sat on the cold, hard stone and wondered when Tibbs would show up. Knight had no doubt that Tibbs would set out on his trail, eventually, but at what level of success he could not guess. The young deputy was headstrong, but he had horse sense and hands that were quick on the guns. Tibbs had proven himself several times, notably when they had faced down old man Usher and his sons.

They set out at twilight, repeating their pattern of cautious activity. Crawling from the cave, Knight tipped his Stetson at Lacroix as the big man grinned at him and wished him luck. They moved off in different directions.

An hour later Knight would learn first-hand of the effort being made to track him down, dead or alive. Moving slowly down an animal trail, he turned a corner but jumped back as a Winchester blasted hot lead and tore up the tree next to him. Three men down the trail had seen him. Knight dove to his left. Then, making a snap decision, he raced ahead and flung himself into a clump of wildberry and rolled across the snapping branches, ignoring the pain as the branches and twigs tore at his skin.

Rolling away, he pulled himself up and stumbled into a thicket. The warm breeze carried the scent of gunsmoke. He paused, hoping to catch a glimpse of his pursuers, when a burst of gunfire on his right forced him into a crouch. He fired quickly at the sound of boots crunching branches. Although he couldn't see through the thicket, he knew that only a few feet separated him from his attackers.

A figure stumbled from the brush, obviously wounded and bleeding badly. A second man followed him, lurching toward Knight and levering his Winchester, spraying the area with a lethal burst of fire. One of the wounded men cursed loudly.

Knight flung his rifle up and triggered a round that exploded the man's head. Keeping his rifle steady, he sighted down the barrel and pinpointed a spot midway down the other man's body as he came into view. The man was too weak from his wound to move out of range. Knight finished him with a shot to the chest.

The dying man had dropped to his knees and spat blood. Knight took the scene in at a glance, steeling himself before firing again. He was aware of the smell of gunsmoke hanging in the air from his Winchester, the scent of the dying man's blood, the arrogant manner in which the dying man spat in Knight's direction. He was aware of all this as his finger curled on the trigger when movement in his peripheral vision caught his attention.

A volley of rifle fire sent Knight scrambling backwards. A bullet nicked his arm, stinging like a hornet. His mouth was dry and his pulse was pounding in his temples. Another bullet nicked his boot.

More men had come up the trail, seen the dead men, and began firing into the brush hoping to kill Knight.

Knight had a glimpse of a man and fired two successive shots at him at precisely the moment he turned to see what the hell was going on behind him. Both shots struck the man in the face. Someone had come up behind him. He heard the man gasping for breath. Knight spun wildly, believing in that instant that he was doomed.

He shot the man quickly, levering and firing until his rifle was empty. The man screamed as he was blown out of the way by the impact of the bullets.

Knight began running.

The place had gone quiet. Too quiet. Booted steps sounded behind him. Before he could react, a man turned the corner and nearly stumbled into him. The man was wiry. Although he was armed with a Winchester, he was smart enough to throw a wicked left fist that nearly took Knight's jaw off. The punch rocked Knight on his heels. Then the man bulled into him, dropping his Winchester as Knight chopped at his arms with the butt of his rifle.

They engaged in a hammering battle. The man's fists landed on Knight's head and arms; a boot struck at his inner thigh. Swinging the Winchester upwards with terrific force, he caught the man on the chin with a blow that crossed his eyes. Grunting, the man slumped forward and, just as swiftly, Knight brought the stock down on the man's spine at the base of his neck. The body slumped soundlessly. The blow from the Winchester's rifle stock had probably been fatal, snapping the man's vertebrae.

But luck was not on Knight's side.

Knight struck out wildly, trying to put distance between himself and the men that had come off the trail.

In a moment, he realized that he was surrounded. Seeing a man come into view, he pulled his Colt free of the holster and the man, seeing this, raised his arms as if the action might prevent the .45 slug from tearing into him. That was his last conscious action. Knight dropped to his knees, holstered the Colt and re-loaded his rifle, plucking the cartridges from his belt and thumbing them into the magazine as quickly as possible.

There were voices and sounds in the underbrush. Forcing his way past another blackberry thicket, Knight encountered an open space of birch trees and began running.

It was no good. They had seen him. Voices rang out in alarm. A bullet slapped dismally into a birch tree, showering him with flecks of bark.

There was scant cover among the trees, but enough that Knight could crouch low and fire at an angle. He took aim at a gunman and let one bullet rip his shoulder apart. The man screamed in pain. The man fell, rose again, and stumbled toward Knight.

The man was bleeding heavily, his face sweating profusely. Eyes widening at the sight of Knight and his Winchester, the man lifted his gun a second too slow. Knight's Winchester split the man's chest apart.

A second later a fusillade of shots cut apart the trees surrounding Knight. Bits of wood and stale dust sprinkled the air. Then Knight was moving again, dodging and rolling between trees.

They were after him soon enough.

He ran, dodging between trees just as a burst of gunfire stitched holes in the treebark. This was followed by a blast of fire from several Winchesters. There were shouts and curses, some garbled, and at least one from a man in pain. Knight's Winchester had a sting.

He was tiring, and his wounded arm was throbbing. He could smell his own blood. Insects hovered in the air around him. He swatted them away, grimaced, and backed further into the trees.

He was running out of time. He had to break free or the men surrounding him would charge and finish him off.

His sense of direction was off. He had lost track of where he was.

Taking a chance, he decided to charge them, firing as he went.

He was sweating when he hit the trail at a full run. With the warm morning sun slanting across the field he remembered a place not unlike this one in a faraway war, his first war; and that had been a life of bugles at dawn and smoke from the artillery fire drifting like ghosts across the Shiloh field, where the incessant buzz of musket fire was as irritating as the mosquitoes that were sometimes so thick on his arms they resembled a fungus. Biting back the memory, Knight shot and killed two men immediately.

He saw another man up the trail with his back to him. A breeze came up and rattled the trees just as the man turned, having sensed his pursuer. Knight's Winchester was up, and he was already squinting down the barrel and pulling the trigger as the man swung his Colt around, but much too late. The Winchester bucked once, twice; two neat shots that slapped into the man's face and toppled him.

Not knowing how many adversaries he faced, Knight proceeded cautiously. The flurry of sound and stampeding boots had vanished. The breeze teased the leaves and the forest seemed to come alive with the lilting tranquility of a summer's day. Then he saw a man cross to his left and he fired quickly. The man yowled in pain, stumbled back, saw Knight and tried to raise his wounded arm. Knight's bullets dropped him in a crimson heap.

Knight burst into a field and swerved to his right. Knight shouted as two men appeared suddenly. This was a shout of defiance, of anger, of a deep atavistic ferocity that only men born as warriors understood. Knight screamed and attacked, using his rifle with unerring skill. Blood burst from torn flesh. Men screamed as their bones were crushed by a flurry of hot lead. The .45 slugs slapped into a man's skull, and he lifted his gaze to the sky as if he were studying something etched on the clouds before leaning over and shuddering as he died.

When his rifle was empty, Knight screamed again and used it as a club. A bullet creased his belly. Yet another man barreled toward him and Knight's Colt was like lightning in his hand, the man's head coming apart in a spray of hair and bone, a pink and gray mist filling the air.

Wounded and bleeding, Knight stopped and crouched on his knees. He could hear his breath pushing in and out of his lungs like a creaky bellows. The stench of death hung in the air. The silence that descended upon the forest suddenly was unnerving. Even more unsettling was the odd sight that greeted Knight as he looked down the trail.

A man was walking toward him with his hands raised. A piece of paper was clutched in his right hand like a flag of truce. The man was calm and unthreatening. He smiled at Knight.

'My name is Castellanos,' the man said, 'and I have a letter for you. I also think I can help you, so why don't we drink some water from my canteen while you read this letter.'

NINE

The man named Castellanos was unhappy. He had taken a job for a man that he realized he disliked. In fact, Castellanos disliked Silas Manchester all the more as he observed the beleaguered US marshal in battle.

The marshal was a brave man. It was obvious to Castellanos that the marshal was unafraid of death. He took chances in battle that few men would dare take. Castellanos wasn't certain if he himself would take those chances if he found himself in similar circumstances.

After Manchester had given him the letter, Castellanos had slipped into the foothills without a word. He cleared his mind of any distractions and set about the task of tracking the marshal.

Castellanos enjoyed being alone. The mountains and forest, he knew, offered a deceptive image. Nature was uncaring of man's plight. He had to be careful in the mountains. Nature could be as murderous as any man could. A flash flood could drown a man in a gully in any of these rolling, steep hills, and Castellanos wasn't about to make any mistakes that would get him killed.

As a boy, Castellanos had lived in Rome with his parents.

There he learned of the gladiators that had fought and died in the Colosseum. His mother told him tales of a brave slave named Spartacus and Castellanos thought Spartacus was a hero. A year before embarking on the long journey that would take him to Boston, Castellanos visited the plains of Lucania where Spartacus fell in battle. This experience was deeply moving for Castellanos. He stood looking out across the sun-drenched hills under a deep azure sky and imagined that final great battle when the Romans finally defeated Spartacus and his followers.

Knight, in some odd way that Castellanos hadn't yet deciphered, reminded him of the legend of Spartacus. Perhaps the resemblance lay in the fact that Knight couldn't be shackled by fear.

Several hours after entering the hills and traversing a long trail into the forest, Castellanos already had a sense that Knight wasn't alone. He found signs of two men, one rather heavy. It took him the better part of the afternoon to sort out the crossing signs and overlapping tracks that would confuse most hunters, even the best ones. But Castellanos wasn't a normal tracker. His father had told him once that he possessed 'a second sight' and this sight, or instinct, provided Castellanos with an edge over most men.

Even in Rome, on those warm summer cobblestones that stretched into endless alleyways and alcoves, Castellanos could track most anyone when he put his mind to it. In fact, tracking a man in a forest was much easier. The earth assisted him, cajoled him, left its own mark as men passed over the mossy surface. A broken twig, fallen leaf, or an indentation where a man had stood next to a tree all told a story that he could read.

He had been in the United States ten long years. His mother and father, last he heard, were still alive and still living in Rome. He had come here to make money – gold – with the intention of taking it back home so that his parents might live in security in their old age.

Silas Manchester had provided such an opportunity.

And Silas Manchester was a bloated pig of a man, uncaring and manipulative. Castellanos deeply regretted taking the job of helping Manchester hunt down the lawman. Fortunately, this was a mistake that might be corrected. He had already received a small leather sack of gold dust to ensure his loyalty, and as Castellanos traversed the forest he plotted how he might honor his commitment without compromising his own integrity. Castellanos answered to himself, and as such his personal code dictated that he keep his word. After all, he wanted to keep the gold dust, not return it.

The solution, he decided, was simple. He had been hired to 'help track down Maxfield Knight'. To this end, Castellanos was content. No violence was required. In fact, while Manchester had offered large sums of money to the man who killed Knight, there was never any discussion of this action being mandatory. As for delivering the letter, this was but a simple thing to accomplish.

Tracking the two men was easy. The challenge was time, which worked against all men. Castellanos wanted to deliver the letter quickly, which wouldn't happen unless he could decipher which track was the freshest.

Knight and his companion were smart. They knew to cross-cover their own tracks and kept to rocky areas whenever possible. Castellanos had determined they had a hiding place up near the cliffs and given more time he could probably find it. As to who Knight's companion was, he had no idea. That mystery could only be solved by locating them both.

He began moving north, sensing from the signs they had gone in that direction. The wild country before him was dense with forest, valleys and hills, all spreading out in the shadow of the treacherous mountains. Cresting a hill, he gazed down into a long valley of pine trees grown so close together they resembled feathered spears lined up and stuck in the ground by some ancient tribe. A solitary eagle swooped high above the trees, its majestic wings spread out on a warm breeze.

Knight and his companion had the advantage. Manchester's men wouldn't travel too deeply into these valleys. There were places here in the mountains seldom seen by any man because of their inaccessibility. The wandering animal trails, hidden glens and furthest reaches of hills thick with pine, birch or oak and maples were seen by none but the soaring eagle, curious bear or wiry cougar. Many a pilgrim on the trek from Massachusetts to the dreams offered by the golden west lost their way; and in some forgotten corner they perished, their bones lost in the pine needles and oak leaves that made a bed of the forest floor.

But Manchester's men wouldn't need to travel to some distant location, as it became obvious that the marshal would fight back. The lawman did not possess the nature of a man who would be comfortable hiding. He would seek out his enemies. He would fight. For Castellanos, this endeared him to Knight as a fellow warrior.

When he heard the sound of gunfire he knew his objective was within his reach. He made his way hastily along the trail, pushing himself toward the sound of the guns.

The letter, he knew, would change everything. Naturally he had read it, and Castellanos thought Manchester had made a mistake by writing it. The letter would infuriate the marshal. From his viewpoint, the letter would have the same effect as pouring coal oil on the dying flames of a fire. Rekindled, roaring to life, a new fire would burst loose from the old embers. He remembered reading the short letter, Manchester's handwriting flowing across the page:

Dear Mr Knight – My name is Silas Manchester and I am hunting you to honor my father's request. Some years ago, my half-brother, the bastard Diego Rodriguez, the son of my father's maid, Manita, robbed a bank, the actions of which resulted in your wife's death when she was trampled by their horses as they made their getaway. I have heard that you followed General Sherman on his March and that you killed Diego with your bare hands. You are a formidable opponent. I have hunted the great lions on the African plains, and my father wished that I do right by his bastard son and avenge his death. I will enjoy making a sport of your demise. Sincerely yours, Silas Manchester.

Castellanos knew these words would anger the lawman. Manchester had no respect for life, and he took his victory for granted. The marshal, on the other hand, would accept the inevitability of his own death and endeavor to take Manchester with him to hell.

Castellanos was forced to remain hidden as he approached the ongoing gunfire. A misstep might result in his being shot by Manchester's men. Rather than join them, he had decided to stay out of the fight, and he would deliver the letter if the opportunity should present itself.

He saw but bits and pieces of Knight fighting, and he appeared to Castelllanos like a ferocious bulldog. He was constantly in motion; like a whirlwind. He realized something then that at times surely worked in Knight's favor – he looked older, weather-beaten, but his physical condition was that of a younger man. His looks were deceiving. This was no aging lawman to be taken lightly.

Remaining hidden, he watched until it was finished and then, without hesitation, he approached the marshal. He offered the marshal the letter and his canteen. He kept his hands away from his gun. The marshal never took his eyes from him, and, even as he read the letter, he sensed the lawman was watching him in his peripheral vision. Castellanos was impressed. When he was finished with the letter his asked Castellanos his name, and then for a pencil. Castellanos had a pencil stub in his pocket and he gave it to Knight. Castellanos watched him curiously.

Knight removed his marshal's star from his vest. He wrote a note on the letter that said, *'I'm coming for you – Knight.'* Then he wrapped the badge and the note in his bloodstained bandana. He gave the bundle to Castellanos. He showed no emotion whatsoever.

'Give this to Manchester,' he said. Castellanos glanced at the bloody cloth and nodded.

'What did you mean about helping me?' The man's gaze was fierce.

'I meant that I will not fight against you. Manchester is not a good man. When I deliver your note back to him then my obligation to him has ended. Perhaps I will join you in battle.'

'I don't need any help.'

Knight walked away without another word, and his footsteps were those of a man moving too slowly, and with too much pain. But he was alive and there would be a reckoning. Castellanos wasn't surprised by the lawman's comment. He had expected it, and he smiled. The breeze kicked up the dust on the deer trail. Castellanos watched him hike higher into the mountains. Castellanos looked at the words Knight had written. There was no doubt in his mind that this lawman would bring death with him when he emerged again from these mountain trails.

TEN

Cole Tibbs watched the two gunmen with an irritated interest. They had been stumbling about the trees examining the ground and trying to impress each other for the better part of an hour. Both men were infuriatingly stupid.

'There's Apaches 'round these parts. That's their sign.'

'They ain't Apaches, Ramsey, they be Suzies. The meanest injuns there is.'

'Claude, you're a damn fool. You mean Sioux, and they spell it with an x.'

'I don't know how they spell it, and I rightly don't care. All I know is there's injuns on our trail. We best be getting back and reporting this to Mr Manchester.'

'We better sit tight and keep looking around. If we can kill an injun that'll get us some extra gold. It don't matter what type of injun it is.'

'It makes me nervous, is all. Just knowing there's injuns makes my skin crawl, and I wanna hang on to my scalp.'

'You ain't got enough hair left to get a squaw excited.'

'Squaws ain't much interested in hair, if you know what I mean.' Ramsey looked around nervously, but Tibbs noted that he never looked up. 'I can feel them injun eyes on me. I just know someone is watchin' us.'

Tibbs resisted the urge to shoot them both. *It was too easy,* he thought, from his seat high in the pines it would be like shooting ducks in a pond.

'Let's amble around a bit and follow this trail,' Claude said.

As they wandered off Tibbs noted with amusement that the trail they were following, whatever it was, wasn't even connected to the false trail he had created hours before. These two had spent a tad too much time on the lonesome prairie letting their brains get scrambled by the sun.

To make matters worse, some ants had come up the tree and were biting him viciously. This, on top of the fact that his choice of tree had put him in proximity with a hornet's nest that dangled from a branch just ten feet from him. More than a few hornets had glided past, either out of curiosity or perhaps assessing him as a threat. It was enough to dampen his shirt with sweat.

Tibbs had been in the tree for over an hour. Way too long. His leg muscles ached, and his rear end was numb. It was time to climb down and either kill someone or find a new place to hide, whichever came first.

Opting to keep his bedroll hidden in the tree, and with extra cartridges stuffed into his vest pocket, Tibbs set out with his rifle and six-shooter, fueled now by anger, which his enemies had learned was the equivalent of any weapon.

He stood for a moment at the base of a pine and glanced about. The soft pine needle bed gave off a heady aroma; the sun, slanting down through the branches, offered up a deceptive view of paradise. The birdsong added gaiety to his surroundings, but the dangerous fools he knew prowled the forest put him on edge. He proceeded cautiously through the sun-laden greenery, circling about to make certain that he was alone.

Once he left the sanctuary of the pine-shadowed hills he felt his pulse beat stronger as he anticipated an attack at any moment. Keeping low, Tibbs made his way once again across the plain of tall grass that bordered the corral. He could hear the horses whinnying; could smell their scent, but he kept his head down and took no chances. It was an interminably long walk, and being hunched over strained his already tired muscles.

He was nearly past the corral and venturing into new territory when voices stopped him. There were guards nearby, and their voices were close. His intention had been to sneak entirely around the camp and enter the foothills at about the same location that he guessed the marshal had escaped. At least he was heading in the right direction.

The voices were familiar to him. Claude and Ramsey, Manchester's devoted clowns, were stumbling toward Tibbs.

'I saw an Injun once in Albuquerque,' Ramsey was saying, 'but he was already dead, shot by a posse of farmers.'

'I'm glad we didn't see any today,' Claude said.

The anger and irritation that had been simmering in Tibbs now flowed to the surface. With his back aching and his cramped leg muscles protesting, he stood up and faced the two men. He felt better when he stood up, the oxygen rushing into his lungs and dissipating the sense of claustrophobia that he'd experienced being crouched in the tall, swaying grass.

He smiled. Claude and Ramsey stopped in their tracks.

'Howdy boys! I am really tired of listening to you two

caterwaul like stuck pigs.'

'What? Who are you?' Claude's eyes popped.

'I'm deputy US marshal Cole Tibbs and you two damn fools need to start running.' Tibbs levered a round into the Winchester's breech.

'You can't shoot us!' Ramsey protested, 'Manchester has fifty men in this camp!'

'I suspect there's a tad less than fifty of you with my friend Max on your trail.'

Claude, perhaps being the dumbest of the two, allowed his fear to overcome common sense, and pulled his gun. His shot flung wide by nervousness, the bullet clipping off harmlessly into the grass.

Tibbs triggered the Winchester, the barrel spewing smoke and hot lead, the shot echoing loudly under the immaculate summer sky. Claude took the bullet on the right side of his chest, just above the bottom ribcage. The impact turned him to his right as the bullet exited from his back at an upward angle. A crimson trail of bone and blood hung like a tendril in the air behind him before collapsing with his body into the grass.

Horrified, Ramsey panicked and charged at Tibbs. Taken by surprise, Tibbs only had time to swing his rifle and crash the rifle butt into Ramsey's forehead. Ramsey took the full brunt of the impact, his eyes rolling in their sockets. Tibbs had put enough force into his swing that the rifle imbedded into the skull a full inch. When he pulled the rifle free blood was welling up in the wound and Ramsey, although unconscious, was muttering incoherently. The impact would either kill him slowly or leave him brain damaged.

The two shots that had been fired were enough to alert

the camp. Wasting no time, Tibbs was crouched low and moving swiftly again through the grass. Once past the camp there was less cover. He paused with his heart hammering in his chest. There were scrub-brush and small trees dotting the landscape, but little else to cover his escape. He was forced to chance it, still crouched, but moving as fast as his aching legs allowed.

He didn't look back. A steady gaze on the territory in front of him was his sole focus. He never stopped. He sprinted from one perceived place of cover to another. A tree, a rock, the swell of a hill, all provided him the opportunity for minimal exposure. He was moving closer to the tree-line and thus allowing himself a better chance of escaping into the thick hills.

He almost made it.

A shout rang out; then additional curses and yells. He'd been spotted.

Bracing himself, Tibbs sprang up and ran head-on toward the trees. Without having looked back he was uncertain as to how close his pursuers were, but he prayed he was out of rifle range.

In answer to that silent prayer a shot clipped into a rock ten feet to his right, and in front of him. Flinging himself to the ground at a point where the ground offered a minimal rise in contour, he jerked about and levered three fast shots behind him. The closest men – four of them on foot – were about a hundred and fifty yards away and crossing the grassy plain near the corral. His shots sent them diving for cover.

Move your ass, he told himself.

He was up and running hard. He started down an incline and up another when another rifle shot pursued him, but this one fell short and wide. He had to keep moving. The danger now was being overrun by men on horseback. The trees loomed closer. Anxiety washed over him. What direction was best once he made the trees?

Another rifle shot shattered the air, followed by curses. His breath was rasping in his lungs; a pain stitched itself up his side. At first he thought he was hit but soon he realized it was his body protesting his exertions. Swallowing a sense of panic, he willed himself to push harder than before. His legs felt tight, the muscles screaming in protest.

Then he was up and into the trees, an all too familiar sanctuary. He was now on the opposite side of the camp. He turned quickly and emptied his Winchester at the men racing toward him. They scattered for cover. Thumbing fresh cartridges into the rifle, he turned and fled into the hills.

There was no trail to follow, so he moved blindly, seeking the thickest groves and tangled green shadows beneath the canopy of swaying pines and maples.

The voices behind him began to diminish but he pressed on. There was no turning back. He had no choice now but to find the marshal. He had a fine tale to tell about getting stuck up in a tree that he felt was certain to bring a rare frown to Knight's face.

At last when he did encounter an old deer trail, he darted into a clearing that spread out and tapered up into the high cliffs. He thought he might catch his breath if he could make the high ground and secure a reasonable position.

An hour later he was sitting with his back to a boulder and looking down at a glimmering blue lake just visible beyond a ridge of maples. There had been no sign of Knight, but that didn't surprise him. Tibbs knew it would be a chore finding the marshal. By now Knight would be riled up. Seeing the marshal angry was something that Tibbs was accustomed to, and he didn't envy anyone on the receiving end of the marshal's anger.

After resting awhile he decided to head toward the lake. He needed fresh water, and there was always the chance he would run into Knight, although he believed it was more likely the marshal would find him first.

Two hours later he was on a northern ridge, having circled about without realizing he had crossed Knight's trail several times, and watching a mountain stream rush downhill toward the lake. He smelled death. There were signs of men – bootprints – and the faint scent of a decomposing body that was unmistakable on the summer breeze.

Tibbs took his time surveying the area and following the stream down the slope. It was tedious work. Eventually he found a body. It was one of Manchester's men all shot to hell. Flies buzzed in the air. Covering his mouth with his bandanna, Tibbs left the body where it was. Although he didn't find any more bodies, he sensed instinctively that Knight had killed several men already.

Halfway down the slope, with the gurgling stream thirty feet on his left, he stopped. Some innate instinct had struck an alarm and he sensed danger. Birdsong chattered from the trees and the sun-laden forest and hills gave the appearance of tranquility, but still his senses warned him of danger.

Then, after scrutinizing every inch of foliage within his field of view, he determined a shape moving about a hundred yards down the slope. The man's outline was partially obscured by the branches and leaves, but Tibbs could see he had a rifle in his hand. Ever so slowly, he shifted his position, once again keeping low, which was causing his over-worked leg muscles to protest. Sweat was dripping under his arms, soaking his shirt. A few seconds later he spied a second man off on the right at about the same distance.

Several obvious facts came to his mind. First, Knight was alive, which wasn't surprising, or else these men wouldn't be here. Secondly, they were taking extra care in being quiet, which could indicate that Knight had succeeded in killing or injuring more than a few of Manchester's men. Without knowing Knight's location, Tibbs was forced to plunge head-long into an unknown battlefield that included every small crevice, shadowed recess, deer trail, switchback and hills and valleys densely populated with trees. The prospect of being killed was at a much higher percentage than Tibbs wanted. He would have to proceed carefully.

But being careful, was one thing, he thought, *and sitting on his ass and doing nothing was another.*

The minutes ticked away as he considered his options. To the best that he could determine, these two men were the only two within his immediate vicinity. Of course, there might be others nearby, but not close enough to make a difference. These two appeared to be sentries watching the creek. It was an obvious location for Knight to use as a swift way of traveling down from the high ridges. He might even have a canoe left here by trappers and hunters.

He took in a deep breath. Still crouching, and with his elbow braced against his raised knee, Tibbs sighted down the barrel and drew a bead on the man closest to the creek. The sound of the cold mountain water tumbling down over the rocks made a roaring sound that amplified in his ears as the tension grew thick. His finger squeezed the trigger.

The man was wearing a brown vest over a blue and white plaid shirt. In that instant when the rifle cracked he saw a puff on the man's belly, just above his belt-buckle. Then he heard the man yowling in agony as he fell.

Shifting his position, he tried to sight on the second man, but he was too late. The man had spotted him and Tibbs, crouched in the mountain underbrush, could smell the gunpowder and scent of wildflowers mingled with the brisk tang of the mountain spring rushing downhill. The twang of rifle slugs hummed past him.

He was up and moving, dodging into the underbrush.

He wasn't fast enough.

A stinging bullet creased his left thigh. Glancing down, Tibbs breathed a sigh of relief that it was nothing more than a flesh wound. He would bandage it later. Levering a cartridge into his Winchester, he slapped two rounds in the shooter's direction knowing that he missed, but forcing the man to jump for cover.

His foot caught a rotten branch that made a sickening *snap!* Off balance, Tibbs fell left, rolling toward the gurgling creek.

Another shot whammed into the dirt on his right. The man had recovered quickly and was firing non-stop at Tibbs. The sizzling lead came splattering through the leaves and tearing up the ground in front of him. Pushing back, Tibbs rolled, clawing his way backwards.

He lost his rifle.

His hands clawed the pungent, mossy earth, his fingers blackened with grime. Gravity tugged him, his own weight his enemy as the embankment gave away and Tibbs was flung backwards into the creek, followed by a blanket of moss and twigs. The cold water slammed into his lungs, knocking the breath from him. Sputtering and flapping unceremoniously, Tibbs, came up gasping for air but covered with soaking moss. In seconds, the powerful stream had swept him twenty feet downstream, his legs buffeted against some rocks. His body was numb from the cold water.

It was the moss that had saved him from being shot. With his body partially obscured by a blanket of moss, the shooter was confused as to his location and so fired aimlessly into the creek. The bullets thunked uselessly into the water. By then Tibbs was well past the rifleman, his Stetson spinning on the mossy blanket as if caught in a tornado. Spinning out of control, he grabbed his hat and tried to right himself and force his body toward the opposite shore.

Cursing his bad luck, Tibbs moved with a turtle's pace toward an outcropping far ahead on his left, but his speed left him only seconds to react. Somehow, and with a surge of determined strength, he moved closer and managed to grab the thinnest handful of branches to halt his momentum.

Hanging by the branches, he inched closer, but the scrub was too thick. He couldn't pull himself on to the shore from here. Tibbs would have to scramble around and try to circumnavigate the overhanging tangle of branches and find an easier place to crawl ashore. But at least he had stopped his momentum. Had he continued he was certain he would have been crushed or drowned.

His boots kicked at naught but fish, and with the water up to his chin, he needed to find a shallow section. Pulling himself around, Tibbs was able to see a shallow stretch about thirty feet ahead, apparent to him by the lighter sandy color wavering in the sunlight. Using the branches, he moved slowly toward the patch of the sandy shoreline.

He breathed a relieved sigh when his boots touched solid ground and he lumbered out of the creek with the water sluicing from his sodden clothes. Instinctively, his hand went to his holstered gun. His spirits darkened when he slapped at the empty holster. He had lost his six-shooter in the creek.

Being without a weapon, especially after barely surviving his fall into the creek, was a devastating blow. His only hope now was to overpower one of Manchester's gunmen and take his weapons.

Tibbs slipped away from the creek and kept himself in the shadowy recesses of the forest. He would have preferred drying off in the sun, but now he had no choice but to remain hidden. He cursed under his breath. He was wet, cold, hunted and without a gun. This, he thought, was not an ideal situation for any respectable deputy US marshal in which to find himself. Max Knight would have yet another good laugh at his expense, that is, if he lived long enough to tell Knight about his misadventures.

What I really need, Tibbs thought to himself, *is a shot of whiskey!*

ELEVEN

During the night he dreamed that his wife walked into the forest wrapped in a blue mist, her funeral dress tattered and rank with mold. But her face was still beautiful, and she smiled at him. The forest had grown silent and about her there emanated a faint whispering sound that he could not explain. She gestured to him, raising her left hand and talking, but he couldn't make out the words. Her golden hair was ruffled by an unseen breeze. He attempted to rise, but his body refused to cooperate. He shouted at her, but by now she was moving past him, a wraith of the night, gliding in a blue mist and vanishing.

Opening his eyes, there was pale light filtering through the forest and, distantly, he heard a voice. He wished that it were her voice, but knowing that it wasn't roused him from a troubled sleep. For an instant he did, however, recall her voice. She had loved reading out loud the poetry of Henry Wadsworth Longfellow, especially from *Evangeline.* She would repeat the lines she loved the best over and over, and thinking of her now he recalled one with astonishing clarity.

'When she had passed, it seemed like the ceasing of exquisite music.'

Far off among the mountains he heard a gunshot and

wondered if it was Lacroix entertaining himself. A cluster of blue and yellow butterflies suddenly burst silently from a crop of grass, and while he wasn't particularly a religious man, he thought that was the closest thing to a sign from above that was possible. What it might mean was beyond his comprehension.

That evening he had crawled under Lacroix's seven-foot lean-to, far off the trail, and tried to sleep. Several hours earlier he'd heard a spattering of gunfire from down near the camp and he vaguely wondered if Cole Tibbs had joined the fracas. His body ached terribly but otherwise he was calm and alert. The exertions he had endured caused muscle pain, and the bullet that nicked him made a wound that was easily cleaned.

Knight thought about killing Diego Rodriguez.

He felt no remorse. He was long past sentiment because in order to survive Knight had been forced to repress any emotions about his wife's death. That had not been easy, not at first. Over time he had managed it, and eventually his grief was replaced by an iron-strong desire to vanquish evil.

His wife had once said to him not long after their wedding day, 'I fell in love with you because you understand why a child's smile is beautiful, and you see goodness in people.'

It was true, but the man that he had been was gone forever. He died the same day his wife was trampled by horses as the five bank robbers made their escape.

Rodriguez was the last one he had hunted down. He beat him to death with his bare hands in an Albuquerque cantina.

The first one had been a man named Garrison, the leader. Knight shot him when he found him working as a drover on a cattle drive. Then the others: the half-breed Sam Coon;

the gunslinger Waddy Hensel and a man named Duggan. They all died fast, and by the gun. But Rodriguez died slowly, with Knight's own knuckles nearly broken from the savage beating he had given him.

He hadn't decided yet how he was going to kill Manchester.

There was no hurry now. He could take all summer if he wanted, and somehow this thought was comforting. But Knight knew he wouldn't wait, at least not long.

In the morning he crawled out of the lean-to and made a perimeter check to confirm that he was alone. There was no sign of Manchester's men, although he knew he needn't travel far to find them. For the moment, he was perfectly hidden.

He decided to connect with Lacroix before commencing his war against Manchester. Let the old boy stew about it and keep him guessing. Meanwhile, Lacroix might have news regarding the gunmen's movements.

By now he was quite familiar with the trails that criss-crossed the valley and he was comfortable as he made his way north and upward into the mountains. He stopped now and again to listen for sounds, but he hadn't heard any gunfire since yesterday afternoon, and that had been near the creek that swept down to the lake. He thought Lacroix must have stirred things up.

He could not keep Manchester's note from intruding on his already troubled mind. He felt victimized, although he wasn't able to say it with those exact words. Perhaps he thought the war had been fought to end this country's troubles, but naturally it hadn't worked out that way. What Knight understood of history indicated that Man was always at war. Maybe it was mankind's fate to destroy itself. That was a grim thought, and it didn't sit right with him.

A maelstrom had struck him the day his wife died. Foolishly believing that mankind's madness was behind him, he had set out to build a life as a farmer, living off the land, and nurturing a family. Her death had taken that all away from him.

The discovery that this land was still populated by random evil acts nearly destroyed him with his grief. Eventually, and only after killing the first of the men responsible for his wife's death, he thought that possibly the best hope for this nation was that our dreams come true a little bit at a time. He could live if he could make that happen for others. He did not think of it as noble or righteous, but simply as something that he was capable of doing. He did not believe then, nor did he believe now, that he was capable of anything except fighting. This was his solitary skill.

He had a purpose, and he understood that purpose instinctively. A man who died without finding his purpose was unfulfilled. The difference between Maxfield Knight and some of the men he faced lay in the fact that they weren't willing to die with a purpose.

With nothing to lose, Knight trudged along a trail, conscious of movement and sound at the periphery of his senses. He slowed, taking in the scents on the breeze and listening carefully to the natural sounds of a morning in a forest.

The grizzly had two cubs.

He had stopped. He watched without moving save for the turning of his head. Straight ahead near a thicket ripe with berries he could make out one grizzly cub in the brush. To his right, but further away, he had a glimpse of the mother. Closer to him, and on his right but almost behind him, the second cub was moving toward the mother.

He didn't feel alarmed, but rather he calculated his options, which at that moment was to remain motionless. None of the cubs were near enough to him to spook the mother, but he needed to remain absolutely still.

The real problem, he thought, almost with a sigh of exasperation, was the fact that two of Manchester's men had suddenly become visible on the trail approximately three hundred yards in front of him.

They hadn't seen him yet, and they were unaware of the grizzlies.

Something caught the men's attention and they stopped. Realizing that they might have spotted that first grizzly cub, Knight sprinted toward the cub closest to him and gave it a swift kick in the ass. Startled, the cub let out a yelp and scampered toward the now fully engaged and angry mother, who had risen up, sniffing the air.

The grizzly mother charged when she saw the two men.

Her speed was incredible. In seconds she had closed the distance and with one mighty sweep of its paws she tore away the man's face. Screaming, the man went down.

Without hesitating, Knight slapped his Colt into his hand and inhaled once, held it, and exhaled as he pulled the trigger. It was a very long shot but it clipped the horrified second man, who had overcome his astonishment and turned to run.

The grizzly took him down. The bullet wound had slowed the man and then the grizzly was on him. A terrible flurry of agonizing screams rose up from behind the hedge where the grizzly clawed and chewed at both men.

The screaming didn't last long.

Already, Knight was running in the opposite direction. He never looked back. All he knew for several excruciating moments was his breath rasping in his lungs and the sweat that soaked his already exhausted body. But he didn't stop.

He also wasn't going in the right direction. He was heading down toward the valley where Manchester's men had spread out in their expanding search.

To hell with it!

Taking time to pause and make certain his Colt was loaded, he determined to take a Winchester from one of Manchester's men at the next available opportunity. His battered Winchester, which he had used as a club, had been discarded and Knight didn't relish being shy of weapons.

He reckoned that Lacroix would come find him soon enough, and that dang kid, Cole Tibbs, was overdue. Knight had expected the kid to show sooner. He would have to talk to him about his fishing habits.

Cutting east, he started toward the creek that rushed down from the high snowy peaks and emptied into that blue lake glimmering down in the valley.

Clambering uphill, Knight followed the gurgling sound of the mountain creek. Eventually, he found the other small bark canoe Lacroix had shown him. It was hidden in the brush and covered with a tarp. He found the paddle under the cover and pulled the canoe loose and cleaned it out. Squirrels and raccoons had made a home of the canoe. The bottom was littered with acorns and twigs, but the canoe looked solid. If it didn't leak he would use it to move downhill.

There was a rope affixed to the bow and attached to a brass hook. Sliding the canoe into the water, he held the rope and let the canoe dangle in the current. A few minutes later he pulled the canoe in and examined the bottom. It was dry.

He climbed into the canoe and pushed off. Cutting the water with the paddle, he adjusted the canoe and swung out into the current.

He immediately realized the current was far stronger than he'd anticipated, and he had difficulty keeping the canoe from flashing downstream. Stroking furiously, he paddled toward shore, having already been jettisoned fifty yards downstream and nearly capsizing.

He paddled along the opposite shore, and, using the paddle as a rudder, he positioned himself just half a foot from the embankment whenever possible. In minutes his shoulders and arms ached from his exertions. Knight frowned. Lacroix hadn't warned him about the stream's current, and Knight should have thought of it himself. This was dangerous, hard work.

Once, spotting an outcropping of rocks in the water ahead, Knight pushed himself up near shore so that his paddle struck sand. With the canoe sitting in the shallows, he gingerly maneuvered past the craggy rocks, the ice cold water slapping at the sharp boulders just inches from the canoe.

Once past the rocks he made better time.

Once, a glimpse of a rifleman downstream had saved him from discovery. Then he heard voices, and laughter.

Quickly, he cut into shore, leapt from the canoe, and pulled the canoe on to the muddy incline.

They hadn't seen him, and Knight, being practical, still harbored a desire to get his hands on another Winchester.

Moving swiftly, he circled around listening to the voices.

He soon spotted two men near the shore. They were relaxed but irritated.

'He ain't got a gun,' one man said.

'Leastways, we don't think he does,' said a second man.

'He didn't look like no marshal either.'

'You heard the boss. He might have friends.'

'Hell, it doesn't matter. Let's find this fella, kill him and get back to camp.'

Knight took a breath, his hand gripping the walnut stock of his Colt, and stepped out of the brush.

'Put your hands up.'

Both men froze, their eyes wide.

'What the hell?'

'Drop your rifles.'

Both men dropped their rifles, but each man still carried a holstered Colt. Experience had already taught Knight what would happen next, but he still had to offer them a chance.

'If you both will be so kind as to unbuckle your gunbelts, I'll be happy to let you live. If you don't I'm afraid we'll have a problem here.'

'A problem here?' one man said incredulously. 'There's two of us. You can't be that fast on the draw! Do you know how much you're worth to us dead?'

'It doesn't matter what I'm worth,' Knight said, 'My gun is already in my hand and I'll kill both of you.'

'You ain't gonna kill nobody!'

Knight shot them both as they simultaneously went for their guns, the blasts from his Colt like thunder in the trees. He stripped their bodies of their gunbelts and picked up both rifles.

Then he went looking for Cole Tibbs.

TWELVE

Castellanos found Manchester standing in a patch of sunlight outside his tent and smoking a thin Havana cigar.

'Would you like a cigar?' Manchester offered, 'The Cubans make very good cigars.'

'No thanks, boss. I have a note for you from the lawman.' Castellanos kept his tone even.

'Let's have it then.'

Castellanos handed him the note. Manchester read it without emotion, his features blank. He folded the note and slipped it into his pocket before blowing a plume of smoke into the sky. He snorted smoke like a bull, the only sign of emotion that Castellanos could determine.

'There is blood on this note. Is it his blood?'

'Yes it is. His knuckles are badly torn. I saw him kill a man with his bare hands. This lawman is a formidable fighter.'

'Is there anyone with him?'

'None that I saw, but there are signs of other men, at least one, but the lawman is the only person I found.'

'What did he say to you? Tell me everything.'

'He said very little. I was lucky he didn't shoot me. He read your letter and wrote that note and said for me to give it to you. That was about it.'

Manchester nodded thoughtfully, looking at the marshal's star. 'You said you saw him kill a man. Tell me about that. What is he like?'

'He fights like a man that isn't afraid to die. I have never seen anything like it. He will stop at nothing and fight until he drops. He's fast with a gun and accurate, and he can fight with his fists.'

'Are you afraid of him?'

'I wouldn't go against him alone. He can't be stopped.'

Again, Manchester nodded. 'I had guessed as much from his reputation, and so I have brought all of you men here to ensure my success. But now I'm truly intrigued by this man.'

'He's impressive.'

Manchester scrutinized Castellanos, who felt a wave of apprehension wash through him as those cold, calculating eyes locked onto him. He couldn't tell what Manchester was thinking, and he didn't want to come under fire – at least not yet. He preferred to see Knight go against this man, and then he would help Knight if he could.

'And his gun skills? You mentioned he was fast, but how fast?'

'Like lightning.'

'How long is the barrel on his Colt? Seven inches?'

'No, I think it may have been five inches, a standard Peacemaker.'

'That's a mistake on his part. A four-inch barrel is best for fast draw shooting from a leather rig. The short barrel levels the gun faster.'

Manchester turned and went into his tent and came back with a gun. 'This is a short-barreled Colt. I am exceedingly fast at drawing and firing it accurately. Knight cannot be faster than I am. I won't believe that, but, of course, we may yet find out.'

'It's good to be confident and especially to have a skill like that. This man will not roll over and die easily.'

'No, I don't expect him to. It's coming down to a matter of willpower.'

'You'll need willpower to beat him.'

'We *all* will,' Manchester said, eyeing Castellanos suspiciously, 'and I expect all of my men to make a valiant effort at killing Maxfield Knight.'

'You bet, boss.'

'Come into my tent for a moment. I have something that may interest you.'

For a second Castellanos hesitated but then reluctantly followed Manchester into his tent. The interior was bathed in yellow and cool inside, with the flaps on both ends open to allow in air. There was a small folding table with an oil lamp, a chair, a cot, and a traveler's trunk reinforced with brass hinges. Manchester opened the trunk and rummaged through it. Castellanos saw silk shirts and an expensive pair of riding boots. He removed two small gilt-edged frames containing daguerreotypes. He showed them proudly to Castellanos.

'Not that many years ago I took up the manly sport of knuckle fighting. I made a great deal of money working the waterfronts in New York. I once killed a man with my bare hands.'

Castellanos looked at the daguerreotypes. They depicted a bare-chested Silas Manchester in a fighting pose, wearing laced ankle boots and shiny shorts.

'Of course,' Manchester continued, 'I have killed in other ways, too, such as hiring a man to do it for me. There are times when a real man shouldn't sully his hands.'

'Very impressive.'

'Maxfield Knight is interesting. He killed my no-good brother with his bare hands. I heard he killed Carleton Usher and his sons in Raven Flats, and he killed Juno Eckstrom in Crippled Horse.'

'They say he's a man without fear, and I believe it.'

'Hmmm ...' Manchester chewed his lower lip, his eyes flicking in his head like butter bubbling in a skillet. It was unnerving to watch. Castellanos thought Manchester was certainly possessed of Satan. 'I may have taken the wrong approach. A man with his formidable talents requires special attention.' Manchester blinked and refocused on Castellano. 'Did you know I hunted the lions of Africa? I have stood in the tall African grass and held my ground against a charging beast.'

'I have no doubt as to your courage, boss.'

'You seem like a man of means,' Manchester said, 'so tell me what kind of man could beat him with his fists.'

'Well, he's a big man, over six feet with broad shoulders. I can't tell his age, but he could be near forty, maybe even younger, but he has the face of an older man. He appears to be very strong. His hands are large, like hammers. There is a great force to his punches.'

'Are you familiar with John L. Sullivan?'

'I've heard of him. A prizefighter, right?'

'He licked Paddy Ryan in Mississippi a few months ago. I was there. One on one there is no prizefighter like Sullivan! He's a bull of a man, tall, strong! By god, a man like that is unstoppable. I have no doubt that Sullivan could easily beat this lawman.'

'Well, boss, I've never seen Sullivan so I'll take your word on it.'

'You do that!' Manchester said sarcastically. 'I fought a man named Patrick Loughman, a tall bastard. He had a reach on me by half a foot and I knew he was dangerous. Do you know how I beat him?' Castellanos shook his head. 'I bulled into him and I let him hit me. Every time he hit me I screamed. That's right, I screamed in his face and charged. It rattled him. Pain is nothing. I shook it off and used my fists like anvils, swinging at him again and again. I gave no thought as to my own comfort. You might be surprised to learn that fight only lasted ten minutes!'

'I think this lawman will have his hands full if you decided to fight him like that.'

'Yes, Knight may indeed be formidable, and I'll admit that he is. After all, he's killed quite a number of my men already, and he's survived much longer than I expected. But now it is perhaps time that I took a stronger hand in these activities.'

'What do you have in mind?'

'A full assault, every man on horseback and armed. And I myself will lead the charge. We'll start tomorrow morning. Meanwhile, I want you to gather the men – all of them, bring them out of the hills and outlying camps. They are to return immediately. We'll all have a good meal and a good night's rest before charging after this infernal marshal!'

THIRTEEN

Cole Tibbs was hiding in a clump of blackberries and preparing to jump the gunman who was coming up the trail. When he saw that it was Maxfield Knight he breathed a sigh of relief and whistled between his teeth. Knight stopped, his rifle ready. Tibbs noted that Knight held a rifle in each hand. The rifle in his right hand was cocked, and although he was holding it with one hand, the barrel was steady. He also noted that Knight had two spare gunbelts looped about his shoulder.

Tibbs stepped on to the trail. 'I see you brought me some guns. I appreciate that.'

Knight lowered his rifle and appeared to scowl. 'I was wondering when you'd show up. I expected you a day or two ago.'

'Well, Max, I was a tad busy. You know how it is. Fishing can tire a man out.'

'I'll show you a good place to fish after this is over.'

'I'll take you up on that. Meanwhile, you've got a small damn army down in that valley looking to string you up. Do you have any idea what this is all about?'

'That I do,' Knight told him what he had learned about

126

Silas Manchester's motivation, and about Lacroix. In turn, Tibbs filled in Knight about his own activities, which elicited a grunt from the beleaguered marshal.

'Where's Lacroix now?' Tibbs asked.

'Probably at his cave, but we're not going that way.'

'And where are we going?'

'We're going after Manchester.'

'Have you prepared your last will and testament?'

'You can stay here, do some fishing.'

'You know I won't do that. But let me ask you this, do you have a plan?'

'We kill everybody in our way. Manchester wants me and I'll give myself to him. Once that happens I'll find a way to kill him.'

'We'll be surrounded by fifty men.'

'Not quite that many. You and Lacroix both helped even the odds up a bit.'

'Even the odds? There's nothing even about these odds. I guess it's a good thing we have the law on our side, being duly appointed federal lawman and all of that.'

Knight gave a snort. 'Take some guns and make certain they're loaded. Now follow me. I have a canoe.'

'You have damn near everything we need except a side of beef. I'm downright starved.'

'We'll eat Manchester's food after I kill him.'

'Nothing like being confident.'

The climbed into the canoe and set off downstream. The creek ran at criss-crossing angles like a series of switchbacks, slowly winding through the hills and into the lowlands. Because of the ongoing thaw high up in the mountains, there was a steady current that made their descent rapid. Tibbs already knew how cold that mountain stream was and he had no desire to get drenched again. Several times they came precariously close to capsizing when they hit the rapids or rocky sections where maneuvering was difficult, but Knight managed to keep them afloat.

Under other circumstances, the canoe trip might have been a pleasant diversion from their duties as lawmen. Tibbs marveled at the wild country. This was a land that seldom had witness; none but the lonely trapper or wandering Indian knew these trails, and the mountain creek swept them through a paradise as beautiful and as uncaring as a harlot's tin heart.

They saw no other sign of Manchester's men. This fact bothered Knight somewhat. He speculated that something had happened they had yet to discover; some change in tactic had occurred that had vacated Manchester's men, at least temporarily, from their search.

There was also no reason to cease in their venture to attack Manchester straight on, as Knight had devised, and so they proceeded cautiously and observant of their surroundings.

Eventually the creek leveled out and Knight recognized the familiar lowlands. They were not far from the lake. Pulling the canoe ashore, they made their way onward, side-tracking to a nearby hill, which offered a better view of the lake and the valley. They saw nothing. There were no men, no sign of a camp.

'This will be a good lake to fish,' Knight said, 'providing you don't get killed.'

'I'll try not to.'

They settled into the hills across from the lake and decided to wait and see if they could see any sign of hunters.

An hour later Tibbs said, 'There's not a damn thing happening down here. Do you think they left?'

'No, but they pulled back. When it gets dark we'll mosey down and see what's happening.'

'That's a good idea, 'Tibbs said sarcastically, 'We can mosey down there and ask them why they stopped chasing you.'

'It's better than sitting up in a tree,' Knight said.

'I knew I shouldn't have told you about that.'

'I just hope you didn't spend all that time up in that tree just to get yourself killed down here on the ground.'

Tibbs noticed that Knight had a twinkle in his eyes and a slight frown on his lips. Hell, if it made the old bastard happy then that was fine.

Three miles away, Lacroix was having a grand time. The mountain man was ambling along a deer path and whistling. He had a new Winchester rifle he'd taken off one of the bodies, and a leather satchel full of ammunition. He had to admit, the Winchester rifle was a dramatic improvement over his old flintlock rifle. Still, he wasn't quite prepared to give away his tried and true flintlock, but under the circumstances the Winchester offered the better chance for survival. He could fire more rounds faster, and reloading was easy.

The Colt revolver offered similar benefits, but he still had his cap and ball 1851 Navy revolver stuck in his holster. Some habits are hard to break. Lacroix decided he couldn't own too many guns, and now that he had extra he would keep them all.

Whistling a merry tune, he wondered how long before

he'd meet up with the marshal again. There was plenty of evidence that Knight had passed through the area. Lacroix found several bodies, including two that had been partially eaten by a grizzly. He had no doubt that Max Knight had somehow been responsible for their fates. The man was resourceful.

Lacroix decided the best approach now was to see what tactic Knight favored, although he suspected the lawman would favor a direct approach. That is to say, Knight would take the fight to Manchester.

That was when he found sign of another man. The boot prints in the mud were of a solitary man being pursued and heading toward the creek. The boots were smaller than Knight's. Someone else was now being pursued, but friend or foe he could not tell. In the end it didn't matter much. If he was an enemy he'd end up dead; if he was friendly he'd probably end up dead anyway. Manchester had set the stage for a bloody showdown and Lacroix sensed that events were in motion that would make that showdown happen sooner than later.

It wasn't long before he determined that Knight and the other man had met and were heading down toward the lake. If Knight remembered it he would take the canoe. It was late afternoon when he uncovered the spot where the canoe had been hidden and saw that it was gone. Good. Knight was using his head, and Lacroix knew precisely where to find him. Of course, without the canoe it would take him a few hours to make it downhill, and by then it would be dark.

No sense worrying about it, he thought.

Lacroix knew the trails by heart and could find his way along through the forest in any type of weather. Being blessed with a stretch of sunny days made his progress all the more enjoyable. At least in that regard they had been fortunate. Some time later, and right about the time his moccasined feet were getting sore, he spotted the camp where Knight and another man were hiding. The sun hadn't quite dropped below the treeline, for Lacroix had made good time. Still, he approached cautiously and surveyed the surrounding area before calling out to the camp. They were in the lower hills overlooking the lake.

'Hello the camp!'

Knight's harsh voice called back. 'Come on in, Lacroix!'

Lacroix ambled into camp grinning. The man with Knight was much younger than he expected, but his eyes told him that he possessed the same ferocity and intelligence that made Knight such a formidable man.

'This is Cole Tibbs. He's finally shown up to lend a hand.'

'Well, it looks like he's just in time.'

'He would have been here sooner,' Knight said, 'but he was up in a tree.'

'Is that right?' Lacroix stared quizzically at Tibbs, who had grown red in the face. 'You'll have to tell me about that sometime.'

'Meanwhile,' Knight continued, 'Manchester's men have all drawn back. They're down in camp and looks like they'll spend the night down there.'

'You reckon they'll come hunting in the morning?'

'Maybe. I'm not really sure what their plan is, but I'm taking the fight to them before sunrise.'

Lacroix whistled between his teeth. 'Well, that's a plan of some kind, and it's better than no plan.'

'You don't have to feel obligated. You've done enough for

me already.' Knight looked at Tibbs. 'Like I was telling you, Lacroix here saved my bacon more than once.'

'I seem to remember saving your bacon a time or two myself.'

Knight grunted. 'Hell, this is about to get ugly. You two had best mosey on. I don't want to feel guilty if you two get yourselves killed.'

'Let us worry about that,' Lacroix said, 'Now if you don't mind I'll sit a spell and maybe get some sleep. I had a long day walking. By the way, I saw plenty of your handiwork. The grizzlies and wolves are eating well tonight.'

'More of that to come,' Knight said.

'I'll stick around, too,' Tibbs added. 'I wouldn't want all of that time I spent in the tree to go to waste.'

Lacroix laughed loudly. 'I am curious about that! I do hope to hear about it before too long!'

The three of them settled down around the small fire Tibbs had built. The three men made small talk about horses, some card games and hunting stories. By a silent but mutual agreement they avoided any discussion of the problem they were facing. Knight had offered up a brief explanation of Silas Manchester's motivation, and then changed the subject. Lacroix didn't push the issue. He appeared content to be with them, and his contribution to the campfire talk was to tell them humorous stories about his life as a mountain man.

They slept in shifts after letting the fire burn down, but the mountains were unusually quiet. There was no sign of pursuit from Manchester's men. When it came time for Lacroix's watch he ventured out and saw from afar the fires burning in Manchester's main camp. All the men appeared to have returned to camp.

All three of them, however, were awake before sun-up.

The sky had turned pale, although the sun had yet to crack the horizon.

Moving out of the hills, they began to wander toward the lake with the intention of crossing the marsh and approaching Manchester's camp from the north-west. They had not gone two hundred yards when they saw a brigade of men on horseback circling the lake. There were also men on foot trailing behind them. The remaining group of Manchester's men was heading toward Knight, Tibbs and Lacroix.

Knight said, 'We'd better spread out.'

A few moments later the gunfight began.

FOURTEEN

Knight moved with greater speed than Lacroix expected. In seconds he had separated himself from the two men and disappeared into a strand of brush. The aches and pains that had plagued him vanished as his adrenalin kicked in and his mind focused on the task at hand. His senses were sharpened instinctively and the world around him seemed to slow down.

The Winchester was at his shoulder in a flash, his finger on the trigger as he sighted down the barrel. He leveled the buckhorn sight on a distant figure on horseback, and fired. The man on horseback, having galloped ahead of the main body of men, had only just come into range. Knight, being highly skilled with a rifle, dropped the man from his horse at two hundred and fifty yards. The man may not have been killed, but he was seriously injured. Knight saw him flopping around in the grass. The other paused, and then rushed forward.

Knight had a fleeting glimpse of a large man on horseback, set back from the group. It had to be Manchester, but he would need to get closer to be certain.

Changing his direction, Knight wanted to avoid being

closer to the lake, where the shoreline would serve as a natural barrier and hence trap a solitary man. He wanted open spaces and the woodland's natural habitat around him for cover.

Lacroix and Tibbs were no longer in view. Glancing over his shoulder, Knight was satisfied they had found cover or were moving in another direction. Knight couldn't help them, but he admired their grit. He couldn't ask for two better companions, and he hoped they lived through this battle.

Three additional men had come into range, all still on horseback. Knight was astonished at their stupidity. Being on horseback made them better targets. He lifted his rifle again and opened fire just as they came into range and two of his shots struck bodies while the third man reared his horse and loped into a strand of trees for cover. Knight calmly reloaded, thumbing cartridges from his holster into his Winchester.

Suddenly a flurry of bullets was ripping apart the foliage near Knight. He dodged, crouched-crawled his way backwards and flattened himself behind a moldy birch tree. A smaller group of about five men had snuck up on his far right. They were on foot and fewer than fifty yards away. Knight was in danger of being pinned down as the main body of men spread out and moved closer. Bullets were now winging his way with regularity. They had all spotted him, knew who he was, and were ignoring Lacroix and Tibbs and concentrating on running Knight to the ground.

These men may not have been the smartest but their numbers made them dangerous. Anger flared in Knight's belly. He wouldn't be taken down that soon, and not that easily.

In his mind's eye he pinpointed the positions of the five men on his right. Then he stepped out from behind the birch tree and took aim, firing rapidly, his rifle smoking hot. Squeezing the trigger, he put two bullets in one man and clipped another in the jaw, which sent a geyser of blood into the air as the man screamed and went down. Another shot staggered a man backwards, his shirt stained crimson as he bellowed in agony. The man's wailing must have frightened one of the other men, who turned and ran. Knight shot him in the leg anyway.

Turning sideways, Knight emptied his Winchester in a sweeping motion toward the main group. It was just enough to stop their advance and give Knight enough time to dash away. The sound of gunfire echoed across the hills. Nearby, he heard the boom of two guns – Lacroix and Tibbs had engaged the enemy from a hillock three hundred yards away. Knight couldn't see them but his instincts told him who it was. He also guessed that Manchester had wisely sent another group to advance from the opposite side, and that was the group that Lacroix and Tibbs were shooting at.

Knight had to admit it was a good plan. Manchester had thought this through and put together a practical strategy. They were attempting to box him in. But Knight wasn't going to allow that strategy to work.

A burst of gunfire tore at the trees and Knight rolled and slid into a thicket that included small trees and a fallen pine. He hoped the pine trunk was thick enough and not rotten so that it stopped the bullets from penetrating.

Crawling the length of the fallen tree, he emerged in a grassy swell and immediately saw two men approaching. They were directly in front of him and partially obscured by underbrush. They hadn't seen him. Knight reloaded the Winchester. He thought with steely determination that if he got low on ammunition he would take cartridges from the gunbelts of the corpses he left behind.

Holding his position, he took aim at one of the men and tracked his movement down the barrel of the Winchester. There was no hesitation on his part when he felt the man was at the right point. The rifle roared and the man's head exploded. He heard the other man curse fearfully as he scampered for cover. Knight didn't have another clear view, so he held his fire. He didn't think the man had seen him and probably only had a general idea as to his location.

Knight crept forward. The man was hunkered down and looking off to his left. There was a moment when everything was still and nothing moved. It was then that Knight lifted his rifle and took aim at the man. When the buckhorn sight rested on the man's chest he pulled the trigger. The rifle bumped back on his shoulder as the .45 slug spun along its trajectory before slamming into the man's shoulder, ricocheting off bone and exiting down through his lungs and out his back. The shot had landed high on his shoulder but the ricochet into his lungs had doomed him.

A gunsmoke serenade proceeded to thunder across the valley. With the hot flame of anger burning in his cold eyes, Maxfield Knight began to meticulously destroy the adversaries he encountered and thereby push himself closer to Silas Manchester. Knight's serenade was a song of death that rang out and echoed across the summer wind.

When a man came crashing from the underbrush, Knight shattered his skull by swinging the rifle like a club. They had come across each other without realizing it, and they were too close to each other to make a rifle shot possible. Knight destroyed yet another rifle with his ferocity, but rather than be bothered by it, he simply tossed the broken rifle aside and picked up the dead man's Winchester.

A crawling sensation prickled across his neck. Turning instinctively, he was able to sidestep slightly as a wounded man lunged toward him, slashing with a Bowie knife. The knife nicked his shoulder. The man bulled into him before Knight could raise his rifle and shoot. The Winchester he'd picked up was torn from his hands.

Everything that Knight did from this moment forward was pure instinct and due to reflexes honed in countless fights.

His elbow blocked a punch as he kicked the man with the toe of his right boot. The man grunted but continued to attempt to pummel Knight. A fist caught his ribs. Not enough to crack a rib but enough to send a signal to his brain that he was in trouble. He took a breath, exhaled, put a right fist into the man's face with his shoulder behind the punch. Knuckles tore skin. The man staggered.

There was no time for anything else. There was a buzzing in the air. Knight realized the buzzing was the sound of gunfire coming perilously close to the two combatants. In his peripheral vision he saw a group of men down the trail firing at them.

Knight's gun came up in a flash and thundered. The man was blown backward, a lifeless and bloody husk for the wolves to feed on.

Then he was diving for cover as a swarm of bullets whipped past him, tearing up rocks and trees. A few bullets even thunked harmlessly into the body of the man Knight had just killed.

Flat on the ground, he sighted down the Colt's barrel and fired. He had to keep them from getting closer until he could find his rifle again.

The rifle was thirty feet away, and in the open. He would be a sitting duck if he went for it. His minor wounds and cuts ached along with his tired muscles but there was enough adrenalin rushing through him that all Knight understood was that red core of anger, hotter than a blacksmith's fire, burning in his veins like hot iron.

He knew how to handle a Colt single-action revolver as well as any man alive. It was not something that he bragged about, and it certainly wasn't something that he wanted to rely on. Knight much preferred a rifle.

He stood up, aimed at the first man he saw and fired. A red spray exploded on the man's chest as he fell. The other men cursed, diving for cover themselves. Knight quickly grabbed the rifle and slid down into a thicket. He had disappeared so quickly after shooting the man that the others were shouting in consternation at each to draw a bead on him and kill him.

He paused and took time to eject the spent brass from the Colt and reload it before holstering it again. He checked the rifle. It was fully loaded.

He heard voices on the trail and the crackling underbrush beneath a boot. Knight was tired of this trail and the parade of gunmen that had welled up as if from a vile spring. He wanted to get downhill, and fast.

Bracing himself, he raced ahead, smashing through brambles just as two gunmen roared at him from the side. He had nearly stumbled into them but for once the men had reacted quickly and charged. He kicked a man between the legs so hard he thought he might have permanently injured him. The man lurched forward, dropped to his knees and vomited before rolling on his side while holding his groin and wailing in agony.

Knight barely had time to club the second man with his rifle butt and dash away. Knight felt that his position on the trail was compromised, but he also knew it wouldn't matter much in the end. That was all right with him as long as he took down Manchester.

He heard gunfire in the distance. It was either Lacroix or Tibbs. The gunfire had been about half a mile away. Knight didn't like the set-up. He wanted to move faster and get at Manchester. He cursed, loudly, not caring if anyone heard him.

He decided to hunt the two men that he had fought with. Remarkably, they hadn't moved far from the place where Knight had viciously kicked the one man in the balls. In fact, that man was limping about and muttering oaths under his breath. They didn't see Knight, who had circled around to come up behind him.

Knight shot them both quickly and moved further down the trail.

Half a mile away Lacroix was sitting on a rock with a smoking Winchester rifle in his hands. A man of immense appetites complimented by a long and vast memory, Lacroix recalled sitting in this same spot decades earlier with his father. They had been hungry. Lacroix had fired at a fleeing pheasant, but missed. At the sound of his gunshot a covey of partridge rose to the turquoise sky. That was when his father's shotgun boomed and a bird fell to the grass. His father killed several more birds that day. They ate well, and Lacroix's life as a mountain man had begun. Those had been good years. His father taught him the secret ways of mountain trails; the path of midnight deer and the dens of slumbering bear. He knew these things now as well as any Indian, and the Indians in turn knew him and respected him, although Lacroix lamented he had fewer Indian friends these days.

He had lost his father and his Indian wife to the ravages of time, and he long ago accepted that his bones would become dust here in the mountains.

The arrival of Maxfield Knight had brought some excitement to his solitary existence. While he had no taste for killing, he lent a hand in the battle as best he could, primarily by firing on the scattered gunmen and keeping them confused. For Lacroix, Knight and Tibbs could do all the killing, or all the dying as the case might be, but Lacroix wouldn't kill a man randomly. Besides, he thought, it was too easy. Lacroix knew every nook and cranny of these twisting trails, and Manchester's men could easily be whittled down.

Maxfield Knight was impressive, especially when he drew his gun. Lacroix had never seen anyone pull a gun and fire that swiftly, or with such accuracy. Of course, he had heard about all of the west's legendary gunmen – Wild Bill Hickok, Chance Sonnet, Hank Benteen – but Knight must certainly be the fastest.

An hour passed and Lacroix offered but a small sampling of firepower. It appeared that most of Manchester's men had circled high into the hills and were now clambering down again. Knight was probably leading them on a merry if not lethal chase.

He had lost sight of Cole Tibbs. When the shooting began,

Tibbs had flung himself off to the left and moved downhill. Lacroix had heard him firing for some time, but now the only gunfire he heard came from further downhill and in the direction that Knight had gone.

He reloaded his rifle and, just as he thumbed in the last cartridge, a flash of beige caught his eye on his far right. The moving beige spot flitted in and out of his peripheral vision like an irritating speck of dust. He studied on the floating beige spot a moment before deciding it was a battered Stetson plopped on the head of a gunman wearing a light blue shirt. The beige and blue moved in unison through a strand of birch, which made the colors stand out.

The man was moving uphill and trying to get behind Lacroix. Damn if he hadn't almost slipped past unseen. Lacroix hefted himself up and backed away from his favorite boulder to find another spot from which to shoot. He was slightly chagrined to realize he nearly missed seeing the man. That just wouldn't do.

He moved toward the man, but keeping to the trees, and settled on a mossy hillock between two spruce trees. Lying flat on his belly, he squinted down the barrel and estimated the distance and location where he thought the man would emerge from a cluster of wild flowering brush.

A fat black bee buzzed past seeking clover.

A centipede inched its way across a fallen twig.

Lacroix breathed in and out slowly, sweat trickling from beneath his coonskin cap. He removed the cap, and repositioned himself, holding the Winchester steady.

He saw the man emerge from the brush and look about in a confused manner. Lacroix wasn't where the man thought he was, and he was trying desperately to find him. His actions were almost comical. His head swung back and forth, his eyes wide as saucers as his brain tried to fathom where Lacroix had gone. Hell, it was almost a waste of ammunition to shoot a man who was that easily befuddled. But Lacroix had no choice. The man was too close, his own rifle seeking a target, and in another minute he might spot Lacroix.

Lacroix's Winchester thundered once. The echo shattered the stillness. Bluejays and sparrows suddenly took flight. Some small animal, possibly a chipmunk, scampered away on his left, burrowing into a wavy clump of pine needles.

Smoke dribbled from the Winchester's muzzle as the gunshot's echo mocked itself in the sunlit hills. He saw the man drop as the echo faded into the forest.

Waiting a few minutes, Lacroix finally hauled himself to his feet with a mighty grunt. He wanted to make certain the man was dead. A span of twelve slow minutes passed and he found the body face down and as still as ole Abe Lincoln.

Once again he wiped his brow, and a breeze came up and the oaks and pines made a rustling sound as if they wanted to move, and in that instant the natural sounds of the forest and valley returned. He took a moment and swept his gaze over the valleys and hills. Seen in the slanting golden light of afternoon, the valleys seemed fresh and new. The mountains behind him, limned by the arcing sun, stood out like a majestic sculpture. He heard the birds chattering and scuttle of animals foraging in the thickets, and for a moment everything was as it should be.

There was no gunfire, There hadn't been any gunfire for a few minutes. He studied on the valley and the surrounding hills and neither saw nor heard any sign of a gunfight. Whatever was happening, it had moved farther down and nearer to Manchester's camp.

There was no sense putting it off. Lacroix had to see for himself how Maxfield Knight had fared, and if possible he would lend the lawman a hand.

Life isn't much without some danger now and again, Lacroix thought to himself as he started down the trail.

FIFTEEN

Cole Tibbs was in a quandary. Maxfield Knight had disappeared and Tibbs was pinned down by two mangy curs who couldn't have been any smarter than a can of peas. Ever since he had set out to help his partner he'd suffered one stroke of bad luck after another. It was downright embarrassing.

He was also giving serious thought that all of them were doomed, and, in fact, the only tangible thing in their favor was the fact that Maxfield Knight possessed an uncanny ability to beat the odds.

He attempted to circle around the two men but they were on to him. Disgruntled, Tibbs was becoming increasingly irritated. The two men were wiry. Keeping hidden, they were stalking him from opposite sides and sending over an occasional bullet to keep him ducking. They weren't smart, but by happenstance they had developed a routine that had, at least for the moment, kept Tibbs stuck in a patch of tall mountain grass and wildflowers near a strand of pine.

His nose itched.

The scent of wild blooming flowers was making him nauseous.

Guessing that one of the men was crouching behind a bush blooming with small, white petals, he levered his rifle and emptied the cylinder in a rush of noise and slinging lead. Nothing happened. No wails of agony, no moans of pain.

Then they rushed him.

Tibbs didn't have time to reload the Winchester. Scrambling backwards, he was forced to switch the empty rifle to his left hand while pulling his Colt with his right hand. He thumbed the trigger back and fired a solitary, haphazard shot that stopped them in their tracks. Although his shot was nowhere near them, the two men stopped, firing at him from a standstill. Bullets tore up the greenery.

The Colt had four shots left. Tibbs realized he had to reload that rifle quickly, but he was still exposed. He rolled into the brush and pushed himself downhill. He landed in a prickly bush. The plant's needled leaves scrapped his skin. Another flurry of gunshots exploded into the brush, but wide of him. They had temporarily lost sight of him.

Never underestimate the value of a rifle, he thought to himself.

He holstered the Colt and reloaded the Winchester, forcing himself to breathe slowly. One cartridge at a time. Then he loaded the Colt so that all six cylinders were full. *Hell*, he thought, *it only takes one bullet to kill a man and there's only two of them!* A shot boomed and struck closer. Peering through the brush he saw a cloud of smoke from a rifle. He fired once and this time was rewarded with a yelp of pain. Still, the man was only wounded. Tibbs knew he hadn't dropped him.

To make matters worse, the gunfire had attracted more men. Tibbs saw them coming uphill towards him. Two more men, and now he was between them and boxed in. They were too close for him to escape. In another moment the men on either side would figure out where he was and either flush him out of the brush or ventilate the undergrowth with bullets until they killed him. He was out of time.

There was no choice but one. The best direction, he thought, was downhill because he might have a better chance of losing them in the trees or brush. Only those two men downhill stood in his way. What would Max do? Tibbs knew the answer.

Jumping free of the underbrush, Tibbs let loose with a warrior's yell just like the Apaches did, and ran toward the two men firing his rifle.

He was unprepared for the fact that gravity would lend a hand and he was suddenly lurching at long gaits down-hill at a much faster speed than he'd anticipated. The two men looked up in shock. 'You boot-licking bastards!' Tibbs yelled. His bullet tore a hole in one man's leg, a fountain of blood popping loose like a cork set free of a wine barrel and unleashing its contents. With a torn artery, the man would bleed out. He fell to the ground clutching his leg and wailing.

Tibbs crashed into the other man. They tumbled and rolled, and Tibbs used every ounce of his strength to hang on to his rifle. He wouldn't lose his rifle again. Tangled on the ground, Tibbs suffered a terrible kick as the man lashed at him with arms and legs as he tried to right himself. Tibbs was forcing himself up and trying to bring the Winchester in play when he saw the man's hands lever his own rifle.

A booming shot exploded the man's head as another man came swiftly into view. Tibbs turned toward him as the man raised his hands and said, 'Easy now! I'm on your side!'

Tibbs held his rifle steady and pointed at the man's belly. He was conscious of the twitching body at his feet and the other still form a few feet away.

'My name is Castellanos. I hope the marshal told you about me.'

'He did,' Tibbs said, still holding his rifle steady, 'but why should I trust you?'

'No reason except I would have shot you already if I wanted to.'

'What do you want?'

A shout rang out as the two men uphill came into view. 'Shoot him!' A rifle was slapped to a shoulder and the muzzle flared as the bullet winged toward them. Castellanos fired his Colt at the same time. Tibbs had seen only one other man manipulate a Colt single-action Peacemaker with such speed and skill. In one silent but lethal motion Castellanos had fired and his bullet destroyed the man's shoulder. Tibbs, edging down, had missed being hit by the rifleman's bullet by mere inches.

Recovering from his surprise, Tibbs aimed and fired. The other gunman spun about trailing a string of blood.

'One is still alive,' Castellanos said. 'Stay here and watch my back while I go finish him.'

Tibbs was too exhausted to argue. Castellanos went up the hill warily, but there was a confidence in his stride that was impressive. He also accepted the fact that this man was no enemy. He didn't really know who the hell he was or what he wanted, but he had just saved Tibbs' life.

A few minutes later a gunshot echoed from the hill and Castellanos came strolling down as if he were at a church picnic. He had stripped the dead gunmen of their holsters.

'You need cartridges?' He asked.

'I'll take what you have. I don't rightly know what we're getting into down in that valley.'

'Manchester is a tough hombre. The men are disorganized and scared. This morning Manchester led them on horseback into the hills to flush out your friend.'

'It worked.'

'Sure, but Manchester lost a lot of men. Who is that old mountain man with the marshal? He has a lot of grit, too.'

Tibbs had to grin. 'A fellow named Lacroix that lives in a cave. It's pure luck that Max ran into him.'

'No, it wasn't luck,' Castellanos said, shaking his head, 'for it says in the Bible, 'and I will smite thy bow out of thy left hand, and I will cause thine arrows to fall out of thy right hand.' This is the Lord's will.'

'We'll take whatever help we can get,' Tibbs replied.

Castellanos shrugged and set his gaze on the sweeping valley below them. 'It's quiet. Too quiet. Let's get down there and see if Maxfield Knight is still alive.'

'He is,' Tibbs said.

Thirty minutes later they had walked down and over two rather large hills that Tibbs decided he never wanted to climb over again when they encountered Lacroix waiting for them on a log. The big mountain man was contentedly puffing on a corncob pipe. His cheeks puffed in and out like a fat fish sucking air, the smoke swirling about his coonskin cap.

'Took you boys awhile to get here. You make enough noise for the whole Cherokee nation to hear you a hundred miles away.'

'Well, you don't look any worse for the wear,' Tibbs said sarcastically.

Lacroix chuckled and expelled blue smoke from his nostrils like a bull. Ignoring Tibbs, Lacroix said, 'I know a shortcut. Why don't you follow me and we'll see how this ends.'

They followed him, and while it took them the better part of an hour to rid themselves of hill climbing, Tibbs had to admit the shortcut was easier than the up and down trail they'd been following.

When they came at last out of the hills the heat was simmering in the green valley under an eggshell blue sky with the lingering scent of gunsmoke on the breeze. Maxfield Knight was very much alive and standing in a stretch of tall, wavering grass. Manchester was forty feet away, on horseback. A few of Manchester's men were on each side of Knight, but further away. They were sullen and apprehensive. Here, thought Tibbs, was a lesson in warfare. Max had frightened them with his merciless killing, unnerved them, and survived to face Manchester down. Lacroix went left while Tibbs and Castellanos separated but remained within thirty feet of each other. They heard Manchester say, 'Ah, the cavalry has arrived.'

Knight glanced back at Tibbs and Castellanos without emotion. Then he turned back to Manchester and said, 'Get off your damn horse.'

Manchester took his sweet time. First he took a cigar from his vest pocket and made a show of striking a wooden match on his saddle pommel and lighting the cigar. Manchester dismounted, gestured for one of his men to take the horse, and stood there appraising the lawman.

'You are well named,' Manchester said, 'Like a knight of the western range righting the world's wrongs. How noble.

Men like you and I have much in common. We might have made a grand time of it alongside King Arthur.'

'We have nothing in common.'

Manchester nodded. 'Very well then, let's not argue. Not at a time like this.'

'Go for your gun.'

Manchester shook his head. 'Oh, no, I think not. Such an ending is beneath us both. Why don't we agree to leave such showdowns in the realm of Buffalo Bill Cody, who makes such an entertainment out of fast-gun shooting.'

Knight stared, calmly, not a flicker of emotion showing on his features.

'Don't you agree that we should settle this like men?' Manchester continued, 'I wouldn't have it any other way.'

'Spit it out. I'm tired of listening to you already.'

Manchester unbuckled his gunbelt and let it fall to the ground. 'I'm suggesting that we settle this as only real men could, with our hands.'

'You want to fight?'

'Precisely.' Manchester began rolling up his sleeves. 'I am quite the expert in boxing. I know you must have heard of John L. Sullivan. I am his admirer and you are certainly a worthy opponent.'

'You're as crazy as a loon.'

'That may be true,' Manchester said, 'but can you beat me?'

'Hell,' Knight said as he unbuckled his gunbelt, 'if you want me to kill you with my bare hands I'll oblige you. I killed your mangy brother that way and I'll do the same for you.'

Manchester's eyes flared and the two men stepped closer.

They circled each other as the clouds crossed the sun and sent shadows fleeing across the grass around them. Knight hit Manchester with his right fist. He hit him so hard that those around them watching could feel the impact in their own bones. A flap of flesh tore loose beneath Manchester's left eye, followed by a gout of blood. Manchester was unfazed. They circled each other again, the cloud shadows crossing the earth like some strange, otherworldly spectres urging them silently on. Knight jabbed with his left and snapped Manchester's head back; then he hit him again with a hard right that nearly rolled Manchester's eyes, but still he did not falter. His face was puffed and red, his eyes like black fire. Knight hit him again and again, and Manchester hesitated.

When Manchester finally threw a punch it was the equal of anything that Knight had thrown. His power was tremendous. The blow connected on Knight's head, just above the right ear as he attempted to dodge away. Manchester struck with the speed of a viper. The two men clinched, grappled briefly, and pushed each other away.

Knight sent a flurry of punches into Manchester's ribs that cracked them, badly. Manchester sucked in air, wincing in pain.

'Very good,' Manchester gasped, 'I was not mistaken in my estimation of your abilities, but this fight is far from over.'

'There's air in your bellows, that's for sure. I'm going to knock it out of you.'

Manchester rushed and hit Knight with a left and right combination that staggered him. Then he kicked Knight in the groin and hit him so hard the lawman was knocked to the ground. Tibbs, watching from a few feet away, was shocked. Remarkably, and against all odds, Knight was back on his feet in a lightning move. He landed a solid punch on Manchester's nose, crushing the cartilage. Blood swept from the nostrils and his eyes filled with tears.

'Let me tell you what it felt like to kill your brother,' Knight said. 'It felt good.' And then he hit Manchester again and again. His fists pummeled the man's face. The skin was ruined, swollen. 'It felt good, and you're no better than your mangy brother.'

Another flap of skin had torn loose beneath Manchester's eye and hung down, revealing bone. Showing no mercy, Knight hit that spot again. And again. Finally, Manchester howled in pain.

'You'll take it and like it,' Knight said between clenched teeth. A fist came out of nowhere and with blurred speed Manchester was struck hard and forced to his knees. Knight stepped up and put both hands around Manchester's neck. He began squeezing, slowly at first, and Tibbs saw Knight take in a lungful of air as his hands turned red themselves from the extraordinary pressure he was exerting on Manchester, who had begun to gurgle and sputter. Manchester's eyes widened in disbelief and then horror as his life was choked out of him. The flesh of Manchester's neck was indented fiercely by Knight's fingers. The fingers looked as if they had disappeared in dough. They all heard it when the larynx cracked. Manchester spewed vomit over Knight's hands, twitched, and died. Knight let go of the body.

Looking about quickly, Lacroix, Castellanos and Tibbs waited to see if any of Manchester's men would try anything, but the fight was over for them as well. The clouds had blown away and the sun beat down from a blue sky.

Finally, Tibbs asked, 'Are we gonna bury him?'

'Hell no!' Knight growled, 'Leave him for the buzzards. I'm hungry. Let's go rustle up some grub.'

EPILOGUE

The following morning Lacroix shot a deer, hung it from a branch and gutted it. Tibbs and Castellanos helped skin it, and they cut the venison into steaks and fed all the men who lingered. At Knight's direction, Manchester's gold had been divided evenly among all the men who assisted with the burials. It took the better part of the day to retrieve the bodies from the hills, and when it was done Manchester's camp had become a graveyard.

Knight still refused to bury Manchester, and so at his direction they hauled the carcass to an area that Lacroix knew belonged to the grizzly. They let nature take its course.

In the end, they were disgusted by the tin cans of food that Manchester had brought and decided that Lacroix knew more about eating than any fat man from the east. Lacroix's venison steaks were popular with all the men. Knight saw to it that Castellanos was given an extra bag of gold, which made the Italian happy. On the second morning Manchester's men had all ridden away, except for Castellanos who asked if he might ride a ways with Knight and Tibbs.

'That's fine by me,' Knight said, 'except we have some

fishing to do first.'

Surprised, Castellanos asked why they would want to go fishing after everything they'd been through. To this Knight simply replied, 'Because there's a good fishing spot nearby. Why waste it?'

Lacroix took them to the lake they had all skirted earlier, and they set to the task of fishing. Now that they had their horses there was no hurry. Lacroix made them poles from sapling branches and had the twine and the handcrafted bone hooks in his pouch. They caught some small-mouthed bass late that afternoon but all of them were too weary to carry on much as the evening approached. The sun had surrendered to a line of deep purple clouds that edged in over the treeline like a row of kings.

Tibbs and Knight had numerous superficial wounds that they cleaned and bandaged. Neither man complained. They bandaged themselves up and said nothing further on the matter.

They made a fire and ate the fish and biscuits Lacroix whipped up from Manchester's flour sack. That night they sat around the fire and listened to the man called Castellanos talk about Rome. He was a good storyteller, and he talked about Italy with such passion that Tibbs almost had a hankering to visit Rome for himself. 'There is such beauty in southern Italy,' Castellanos told them, 'that it rivals a beautiful woman. The rolling hills are green and the vines are fat with grapes that will make fine wines.'

The following day they fished in earnest. It was a good day for fishing. They pulled out half a dozen fat bass, and at midday Lacroix pulled out a musky that was so big it could feed a family. In the late afternoon they rekindled the fire, cooked the fish and marveled at the ever-changing lake that looked different but wildly beautiful under the sun and at the foot of the mountains. The wind and sun added a sparkle to the waves and an eagle joined them, swooping low and snatching a fish from just below the surface. They heard its majestic wings swoosh the air as it passed over them.

That afternoon they ate their meal and finished the last of Manchester's bourbon, with the exception of Tibbs who was a teetotaler except twice a year, on his birthday and on Christmas day. Knight remarked he would drink Tibbs' fair share for him. The sun had begun to sink below the treeline when Knight said to Castellanos, 'Do you have any trees in Rome?'

'Sure, we have trees, but not like the trees here.'

'You ever know anyone to get stuck in a tree like Tibbs here did?'

They all laughed, and Tibbs felt himself turning red.

'I treed a coon once,' Lacroix said. 'He stayed in that tree all dang day while I roasted some fat bass below him. That coon got mighty hungry. When he finally came down I shot him and ate him, too.'

The roar of their laughter echoed across the lake.

The next morning Lacroix announced that he was heading home. He had accumulated the guns and ammunition from the victims of Knight's rage, and there was no sense in letting it all rust. There was no shortage of game and he could hunt to his heart's content.

Lacroix shook their hands and invited them to visit any time. He said he'd promise not to blow their heads off with one of his new Winchester rifles as long as they came in slow and didn't bring trouble with them. The last few days had shown him enough trouble to last a lifetime.

Tibbs hated to leave the lakeshore, but they had obligations to the US Marshal's service. Castellanos got the horses ready, and they started out when Knight told them, 'Ease up a spell and follow me in slow. There's a place I need to visit.'

Tibbs had an inkling on what that place was but remained silent. Riding out of the valley they followed the same trail that had brought Tibbs here those long days ago. It took them all afternoon to reach the place that Knight was intent on visiting.

There was a cemetery near a strand of wavering oaks. The leaves rustled on the wind. Knight told them to stay put. He cantered his horse up to the cemetery and dismounted. He tethered the horse to an old picket gate and went to stand near a stone marker. Neither Castellanos nor Tibbs could read the name on the marker, but knew who it was. They watched silently as Knight bent over and pulled some prairie flowers free of the earth. The rough and crushed prairie flowers looked somehow majestic in his calloused hand.

Castellanos and Tibbs heard him say something, but Knight's words were lost on the breeze. Then he set the flowers on the grave and returned to his horse. When Knight had ridden up next to them, Castellanos nodded and said, 'It sure has been a pretty day.'

'That it has,' Knight said.

'Are you ever going to tell me about your wife?' Tibbs asked.

'Nope,' was all that Knight said.

They turned their horses up the trail as the wind pushed

through the tall grass with a sound like whispering ghosts, and together the three men rode into the sunset.